THE FLYING U STRIKES

Center Point
Large Print

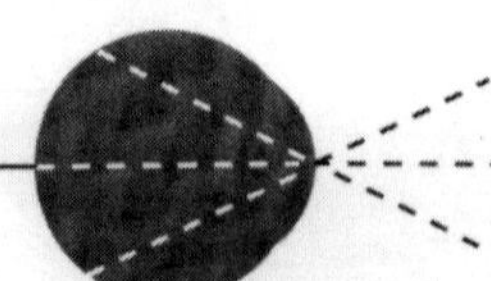

This Large Print Book carries the
Seal of Approval of N.A.V.H.

14

THE FLYING U STRIKES

B. M. BOWER

CENTER POINT PUBLISHING
THORNDIKE, MAINE

This Center Point Large Print edition
is published in the year 2004 by arrangement with
Golden West Literary Agency.

The text of this Large Print edition is unabridged. In other aspects, this book may vary from the original edition. Printed in Thailand. Set in 16-point Times New Roman type by Bill Coskrey and Gary Socquet.

ISBN 1-58547-402-9

Library of Congress Cataloging-in-Publication Data

Bower, B. M., 1874-1940.
The Flying U strikes / B. M. Bower.--Center Point large print ed.
p. cm.
ISBN 1-58547-402-9 (lib. bdg. : alk. paper)
1. Ranch life--Fiction. 2. Cowboys--Fiction. 3. Montana--Fiction. 4. Large type books.
I. Title.

PS3503.O8193F58 2004
813'.52--dc22

2003021318

I

TROUBLE BEGINS

A RAW MARCH WIND SUCH AS ONLY THE HIGH prairies ever know poured like ice water over the bald benchland that forms a part of the Flying U range. It roughened the hair on the two saddle horses; it tossed their manes and it whipped their tails around their hocks as they loped down to the bluff edge where the rough country began.

Chip Bennett, younger of the two riders, broke a silence of half an hour. "Those horses will be hugging the brush on a day like this," he said, and drew a hand across his smarting eyes.

"That's right," Weary Davidson agreed. "No use combing the benches today. Mamma! That wind sure does go through a fellow! What say we swing over to the left here, Chip, and kinda bear off more toward the river? They're in the breaks, that's a cinch. We've had this wind for four days. I look for 'em to be watering along Rabbit Creek where there's lots of shelter."

"That's what I was thinking." Chip hunched his shoulders within his sour-dough coat. "We can make it down off that point over there easiest."

With one accord their rein hands twitched to the left and the horses obeyed that slight pressure against the right side of their necks. Instant relief was felt from that biting wind, now pushing hard against their backs instead of flat against their right sides. The tear lines dried upon their cheeks. They let their horses down to a walk, pulled off their gloves and sat on them while they rolled and lighted cigarettes. Neither spoke again. Neither was conscious of their long silences which held a satisfying companionship not to be broken by idle chatter. They were content and that was enough.

Overhead the sky was blue and the sun shone with a spring brightness. After a while, when they turned off the sloping point of the bench and picked their way down a rocky gulch, a pleasant warmth surrounded them. Here the cold wind could not search them out. Riding ahead, Chip leaned suddenly from the saddle and plucked a crocus from the bank. Straightening again, he took off his hat and tucked the downy stem beneath the hatband in front, and set the hat atilt on his brown head. With his overcoat unbuttoned, Weary rode slack in the saddle, whistling an aimless little tune under his breath.

Down in the sheltered coulee it was spring. A few fat prairie dogs were already bestirring themselves, hunting grass roots or running from mound to mound to gossip with their neighbors. As the two cowboys approached, a shrewish chittering met them, the village inhabitants all standing up on the mounds with their front paws folded like hands. Abruptly they lost courage however and ducked down into their holes, the flirt of their stubby tails as insolent as a thumbed nose.

Out of that coulee and up over another small bench went the riders, the chill wind hounding them over the high ground only to give up the chase when they dipped down into the next hollow. In spite of their seeming casualness, their questing glances went here and there, scanning each wrinkle and hollow that lay exposed to their gaze. The bunch of horses they were hunting might be almost anywhere in this kind of weather.

Weary suddenly pointed a gloved finger. "Ain't that a dead critter down there by that brush patch? Looks like the wolves have been at work down in here."

"Not one but six carcasses down there," Chip answered him. "We better go take a look. If it's wolves, they sure have been holding high carnival down there." He reined his horse straight down the slope toward the spot, Weary after him.

It was so steep that when they struck a shale patch both horses slid on their rumps for some distance. But they made the bottom without mishap and rode down to the thicket. A deep bowl of a place it was, the center a jungle of wild berry bushes growing in such luxuriance as would indicate a spring close by. On the sunny side of the thicket lay a group of carcasses, evidently some time dead.

The two rode up and stopped, staring about them. "Mamma!" gasped Weary. "Looks like here's where the wolves have held an old-timer's reunion. Six beef critters pulled down all in one bunch! Now what d'you know about that?"

"Not half as much as I'm going to know before I'm through," Chip retorted. He stepped off his horse and walked over to the first carcass. With his hands on his hips he stared down at the unlovely heap for a minute, then walked on to the next and the next. He turned back and looked at Weary, standing just behind him.

"Shot in the head. The whole damn bunch," Weary answered the look. "You saw that, didn't yuh?"

"I'd tell a man I saw it. Take a hold, here. Let's see the brand—if they left one."

They caught hold of the mauled and shriveled hide where the hind quarters should have been and flipped it over. The brand was the Flying U, and as they went from one to the other, they verified the brand on each. Six Flying U beeves, still showing the bullet holes in their heads where they had been shot down. And while the fore quarters had been half devoured by wolves, the hind quarters had been skinned out of the hides and carried off.

"Beef rustlers," said Weary, as they returned to their horses. "I sure would like to know who pulled that stunt. Looks to me like they either want to advertise the fact they're after the Flying U or else they don't give a darn. Never even took the trouble to cut out the brands, you notice." He looked at young Bennett. "That mean anything to you, Chip?"

"It certainly does. After that trouble last summer with Big Butch's outfit, it means they're making war medicine again. I was wondering what made 'em so damn peaceable; after losing four men in that fight we had, it looked to me like they'd take another whack at the Flying U, just to break even." Young Bennett frowned down at the nearest heap of bones and hide. He did not add what loomed blackest in his thoughts: that he himself, with a personal quarrel to settle with one of Big Butch's men, had really brought the Flying

U into the trouble with Butch Lewis' outfit.

He hated to admit it, even to himself, but it was true. He had been looking for his brother, up in this country along the Missouri, and had run into mystery and trouble in his search. Brother Wane was dead—murdered, he believed, in spite of assurances that Wane's death was an accident. And one day he had seen one of Butch Lewis' men riding Wane's horse and saddle, the EB brand botchily changed. Well, he had gone after Cash Farley and got the horse away from him, but in the long run the Flying U had paid high for that reckless adventure. Paid with a hundred head of saddle horses stolen out of the pasture in Flying U coulee; paid with a bullet in Jim Whitmore's leg, beside. And now, good old "J.G." was paying again, with good beef slaughtered on the range, his brand left insolently as a challenge and a defiance to the outfit.

It was plain enough to Chip Bennett. Last summer the trouble had culminated in a hair-raising afternoon when he had been hunted from rock to rock by Cash Farley and his cronies with rifles. Well, his own rifle had taken up the argument pretty decisively. Fighting for his life, he had held them off until the Flying U boys had come to the rescue—Weary, here, was one of the first to arrive. He knew just what these carcasses meant. Big Butch Lewis was taking up the fight where it had been dropped last summer.

Then Weary dissented from that conclusion. "Big Butch might be makin' war medicine, like you say, but not this way. It's somebody else rustling beef off us."

"I'll bet it's Butch, building up another scrap with

this outfit," Chip said glumly. "Come on. I'll bet we'll find more."

They mounted and rode up out of the little basin and over into the next gully. Sure enough, here were several more, all showing the Flying U brand. In another deep coulee they counted twelve carcasses, and with a stubborn thoroughness young Bennett insisted upon examining each one. Flying U. Not one Hobble-O, though plenty of Shep Taylor's stock ranged in here, as did the Lazy Ladder and a few nester brands. Whoever had butchered these cattle certainly picked his brand with care.

All that afternoon they rode through the sequestered places where Flying U cattle had wintered for sake of the shelter. Hundreds of them were grazing there now, looking fat and strong after the long months of cold. Once Weary remarked that the calf crop ought to be a banner one that spring, but Chip only nodded agreement. Banner calf crops could not alter the fact that his own personal enemies were taking their grudge out on the Flying U and that there didn't seem to be anything much that he could do about it.

They found the bunch of horses they were after and hazed them up on the bench and headed them toward the ranch, then continued their scrutiny of the coulees and gulches that webbed the strip lying between the level benches and the Badlands along the river. Again and again they came upon the mutilated remains of Flying U stock, and judging from what was left, they guessed them all to be young beef steers just under shipping age.

“Good beef,” commented Weary, “but damned expensive eating, just the same. J.G.’s going to be shy a couple of carloads of beef next fall. And believe me, that sure runs into money!”

“I know it,” growled Chip. “You don’t have to rub it in.” In a little memorandum book he was keeping a methodical tally, and the mounting figures stunned him into silence. Just as sure as the sun was shining, the Flying U was being baited into a fight. No use talking about it—words wouldn’t change the facts, no more than they could ease his heartsick feeling of responsibility in the matter. No, there wasn’t much to be said about it: Jim Whitmore was being stolen blind. It had been going on all winter, almost under their noses. It was still going on. Some of these last butcherings they had found looked fresh. A couple of days old at the most.

“Whoever it is, they’re sure doing a land-office business in beef,” Weary remarked, as he lifted himself into the saddle after inspecting the last and freshest one. “I can’t think it’s the Butch Lewis bunch, though. They’re supposed to be in the horse business. I never heard of them peddling beef.”

On his horse, Chip concentrated upon the little book open in his hand, adding a column of figures twice; once from the bottom up, then with an incredulous oath, starting at the top and going on down.

Weary watched him over the cigarette he was making. “How many, Chip?” he queried, glancing down at the match and turning it head down, to draw it along the fork of his saddle. “I started to keep count in my head—but hell, I give it up ten miles back."

"Eighty-three," young Bennett told him without looking up. "It doesn't seem possible—"

"*Eighty-three?* That's damn near three carloads of beef the sons uh Satan have got away with. Yuh realize that? And half of it plumb wasted and fed to the wolves!" Weary blew smoke from his nostrils with the snort he gave. "Say, J.G.'ll go straight in the air when he hears about this. . . . Well, we might as well be getting back."

He reined toward the steep slope of the gully, Chip following behind. The horses climbed nosing out their footing as they heaved themselves over the worst places in rabbit hops. On the long hogback ridge that sloped gently up to a thicket-crowned swale just under the bench top, Weary looked back down into the gully.

"Mamma! That's a lot of meat, Chip," he observed in a shocked tone. "J.G.'s a lot poorer than he thought he was."

"It'll be paid for," Chip said shortly, though he could have had no clear idea of just how it would be paid. Uneasily he was adding the little column of figures again, as his horse walked steadily up the slope. He was hoping that he had made a mistake, but there it was. Eighty-three which they had found and inspected; how many more there might be hidden away in this broken country he had not the courage to guess. They hadn't found them all; he knew that.

He had put away the book again and was fumbling for the button to close his flapping overcoat, when the heavy canvas gave a vicious twitch in his fingers. It wasn't the wind. He glanced down at his coat, gasped with astonishment and spurred ahead into the shelter of a brush patch. And as he did so, the faint *pow-w* of a rifle shot came to his ears, the sound dimmed by distance and almost whipped away entirely by the gusty howl of the wind.

II

CHIP TAKES THE HINT

WEARY TURNED WITH A TWINKLE IN HIS EYES AT THE sudden haste Chip displayed. "What's the matter? Got a snake bite?" he inquired mildly, knowing full well that the hardiest snake would scarcely be abroad in March.

"No. A flea," Chip came back at him instantly, while he pulled up to search the gully with his eyes.

Big Butch without a doubt, he was thinking; Big Butch or one of his men, trying to get even for Cash Farley. Not even a wisp of smoke across the gulch gave a clue to his whereabouts, and to go back and search for him was worse than useless. He might be anywhere amongst the rocks and brush on the farther wall, and to reach him except with a bullet was practically impossible. No use saying anything to Weary about it, either. Might stir him up to want to go hunting the shooter—and while they were getting into the gully and across to the other side, they would be easy targets. Chip had enough experience with that sort of thing to feel no desire whatever to make the attempt.

It was plain Weary had not heard the shot. "No more carcass hunting today," he declared, misinterpreting Chip's pause. "You couldn't get me down into another coulee on a bet. I've got enough on my mind with them eighty-three we already counted. Come on. We'll pick up them horses and hit for home. That's work enough for today, if you ask me."

"I'd like to get one crack at whoever's doing it," Chip said, reining reluctantly alongside. "I'll sure do it too."

"Not here and now you won't. Gosh, that wind's a corker, ain't it? For the lordsake, Chip, come on!"

They overtook the horses just as they were swinging off toward another coulee to get out of the wind, and hazed them along at a hard gallop across the bench and down a gravelly ridge. Heads bowed to the bitter wind, they rode doggedly, eyes red and smarting. On this bare slope the gale gouged loose patches of gravel and flung it in clouds high into the air. Small pebbles flew like hailstones, pelting horses and riders alike. The short grass, its curly blades showing green at the roots, whipped flat to the ground.

Hating to face the cruel blast, the loose horses spread out where they could and tried to dodge back to more sheltered places they knew; but two shrill-voiced demons seemed always just where escape was most easily blocked, and outguessed them, outran them, turned them back into the teeth of the wind. Manes and tails whipping, ears laid back, they tore down the hill, blinding their captors in the dust their unshod hoofs flung up for the whooping gale to seize and sweep along; a wild and picturesque flight which a Russell would have loved to paint.

The brushy bottomland of Flying U creek received them at last. A hundred yards from the new pasture fence below the camp Chip spurred ahead to open the gate. The half broken horses shied, snorted in pretended panic and steamed through the opening, and Weary swung off to drag the wire-and-pole gate into place again and fasten it with the chain loop.

"What'll we do, Chip—tell J.G. right away about them butchered steers, or wait maybe till morning?" he wanted to know, as he galloped up alongside again.

"Why wait? It's got to be told."

"Yeah, it's got to be told. But I thought we might maybe give the Old Man one more night's sleep before he knows it." He leaned and spat wide of his horse. "Just as you say, though."

Chip rode ten rods at a walk, his hands clamped over the saddle horn, his slim young body swaying slightly in perfect rhythm with his horse's steps, like a dancer catching the beat of the music that is in his blood. He drew his teeth gently across wind-chapped underlip while he came to a decision and suddenly he looked at Weary.

"It's something more than slaughtered beef," he said, and caught the edge of his coat between thumb and finger, turning it out for Weary to see. "That's why I jumped my horse behind the brush. Pretty good shooting, when you take distance and wind into consideration. Whoever did it, he was so far off you didn't hear the shot. I did, because I happened to be listening for it."

"Mamma!" gasped Weary, leaning to squint at the round hole with its brownish rim. "Took you all this while to jar loose a word about it, huh? You sure are a mouthy guy!"

"What was the use? We couldn't get at him. He was over across the gully, cached somewhere in the rocks. Been watching us, most likely. The funny part is that he waited till we were both almost out of sight before he made up his mind to take a shot at us."

"That ain't funny," Weary corrected him soberly. "That's luck."

"That's enlightening, you mean. Shows who it is he really wanted to get."

"You?"

"Who else? He let you get by into the brush. For that matter, he let us both get out of the gully and up on the ridge where we couldn't very well take after him—which shows he didn't want a gun battle on his hands. All he wanted was to pot me while he had the chance."

"I wish," said Weary complainingly, "you'd of said something about it at the time, Chip. I'd 'a' gone back after the dirty son-of-a-gun."

"And that," Chip retorted, "is exactly why I didn't say anything about it."

"No," Weary made sarcastic comment, "I suppose you'd let him beef yuh like he did them steers, before you'd condescend to mention the fact. You sure are a self-sufficient cuss, but some of these days you'll bump into the fact that you can't buck this game all by your lonesome."

"Yes?"

"Yes! Daw-gone you, *yes!* Sometimes, Chip, you make me so damn mad—"

"Because why? I haven't done a thing, so far."

"Mamma!" sighed Weary. "Ain't I just been telling yuh? It's you trying to play a lone hand that started all this ruckus in the first place. If you'd passed the word to us boys, that day at Cow Island, instead of foggin' off after Cash Farley by yourself, you wouldn't be getting buttonholes cut in your coat like this, maybe."

"I don't see how you figure that. I got the horse I went after, didn't I? If I'd waited to holler for help—"

"You'd of showed brains," Weary finished the sentence, according to his own ideas. "We'd likely have tangled with Cash right then and there, and chances are he'd of been laid away. That would of settled it. Instead of that, you let him go and frame up ways of getting even. Now the Flying U's out two, three carloads of beef, to say nothing of that bunch of horses they got away with last summer."

"Rub it in, why don't you?" Chip inquired acrimoniously. "You've changed your tune, seems to me. I thought it wasn't the Butch Lewis gang doing all this?"

"Well, it ain't." Weary's face relaxed into a brief grin. "I'm just carrying out your argument, is all—running you into a corner with it. It's this idea you've got of bowin' your neck and going head on after a thing. I'm showin' you how you pan out when you try and take things into your own hands. If this is Big Butch's work, which it ain't by a long shot, and if you're chump enough to try and settle with him alone, which you couldn't do, why, I'm tellin' yuh right now, Chip, that Big Butch'd just made one bite of you."

"Oh, go to hell!" snorted Chip, and pulled the big collar of his sour-dough coat higher around his ears as he spurred his horse into a faster pace.

"If I do, I'll sure have you along for company," Weary retorted. "You certainly are about as bull-headed a cuss as I ever met up with."

To that statement Chip deigned no reply, and with ill feeling between them for the first time in months, they rode in silence to the creek, splashed through a paper-thin glaze of new ice and loped up to the corral. In silence they unsaddled, stabled their horses and went crunching through freezing mud on the path to the cabins. Where the trail forked near the bunkhouse, Chip swung off toward Jim Whitmore's cabin, conscious of Weary's surprised glance as he went on.

An uneasy feeling that Weary was right, that nothing would be gained by telling J.G. now of his loss, slowed Chip down to a laggard pace which halted beside the little square window beside the door. Glancing in, he saw J.G. lying on his bunk asleep, his lips gently puffing in and out with the subdued snores he emitted. The lamplight shone on the bald patch coming on his head. . . .

Seconds ago the bunkhouse door had slammed behind Weary. Chip looked that way, looked in again at the window. When a cowboy is in doubt, he usually rolls a cigarette—or did in the days before the tailor-mades. Chip took his time doing it, his thoughts dwelling miserably upon the trouble and loss he had caused Jim Whitmore in the months since he had come riding north, looking for his brother Wane. Discord and enmity seemed to have followed him like a cloud of hungry mosquitoes.

There was the trouble at Cow Island, when he had been all but hung on a trumped-up charge of stealing his own horses. Dave Burch and Tom Shaner, glorying in their authority as leaders of the Vigilantes, would never forgive the Flying U for making them back down.

And there was the Butch Lewis outfit—or maybe his name was Butch McGoon; Hec Grimes at Cow Island had called him that. His trouble with Cash Farley, one of Butch's men, was the direct cause of all this beef stealing now. Chip would have sworn to that. All through the summer he had piled up trouble for good old J.G., and now he had to go in and tell him of this last outrage. His cigarette was smoked down to the stub before he could bring himself to the ordeal; a bitter thing to face—but it wouldn't be better for the waiting.

III
A MAN-SIZE JOB

HIS CIGARETTE WAS SMOKED DOWN TO THE STUB WHEN he heard a prodigious yawn inside. He pinched out the fire in his cigarette, ground the stub carefully under his heel and opened the door.

He was not long in the cabin. When he came out, his eyes held a bleak look they had not worn before. Opposite the window he halted again for a glance inside—and flinched at what he saw; J.G. sitting on the edge of his bunk, absently crowding fresh tobacco into his pipe, while he stared unseeingly at the wall before him, looking somehow years older than he had ten minutes ago, when he lay peacefully asleep after a hard day in the saddle.

One look and a sharp indrawn breath, and Chip turned away and walked with squared shoulders to the bunkhouse. Instant silence fell upon the place when he opened the door. The Happy Family, evidently deep in discussion a moment before, sat in awkward self-consciousness as he came in and pushed the door shut with a twist of his shoulder. Eyes followed him to the stove, watched him while he stood there with his back turned upon them, warming his hands. For all the sign he gave, the room might have been empty—which was the cold aloof way he had when life struck at him too harshly. And for the moment no one seemed willing to batter against that wall of silence with which he held them off.

Then Weary, combing his thick dark hair before the small mirror that made him crouch down to see himself in it, he was so tall, turned with the comb poised just over his right ear.

"Well, what'd he say, Chip?" he asked, with a complete disregard of any past disagreement. "Jar loose a little information, can't yuh? What's J.G. think about it?"

"I didn't ask him what he thought."

Cal Emmett, sure to blunder into touchy subjects, gave a constrained laugh. "Hear you've been annexin' some extra buttonholes, Chip."

Chip half turned toward him. "Yes? News travels fast in this country." His tone was tart.

"Meaning I'm too damn gabby," sighed Weary. "Sure, I told the boys about that. Keep 'em off the sky line, maybe, till we can glom the jasper that done it. Take a look at that hole, boys."

He came over to Chip, looked straight into his moody hazel eyes with his sunny blue ones, and twitched the sheepskin-lined canvas coat open. "See that? If Chip had been setting three inches forward, that bullet would of bored plumb through his lungs and heart sideways. That's—"

"His *what?*" Cal Emmett chortled, to hide the shock he felt.

"Oh, he's got a heart, all right. You ask that family of silver-maned horses of hisn." Weary gave the coat an affectionate yank and let Chip go. "Mamma! A little better shooting, and I'd 'a' had to pack him all the way home against that wind. You can't," he plaintively explained, "drive a bunch of horses worth a damn when you're packin' a corpse on a led horse behind yuh."

From the corner of his eye he saw Chip grin at that oblique acknowledgment of gratitude, and a tension left Weary's mouth. "The great and burning question now is, who do we know that's as good a rifle shot as that? Three hundred yards, if it was an inch, and a high wind to allow for."

"Aw," Happy Jack croaked unbelievingly, "there ain't nobody that good a shot. I betcha he was aimin' at somep'm in the gully and shot over."

"Shep Taylor's a wiz with a rifle," Ted Culver offered. "Been sellin' beef all winter too. Yuh mind, Cal, we met him and Snuffle haulin' two four-horse loads out to the fort. That was about a month ago, when we was comin' out from Dry Lake."

Weary gave a quick shake of the head. "Wouldn't be Shep. Way I figure, it's some of them nesters that moved in last fall down along them creek bottoms. Shep Taylor's an ornery cuss to work for, but he's straight. I'd bank on that."

"Just the same, I wouldn't put it past the Hobble-O," Ted persisted. "By gosh, if I'd of known what was goin' on, I'd sure as hell clumb up and took a look in them wagons. I'll gamble there was more hind quarters than there was front."

At the washbasin Chip lathered hands and face with a cake of yellow soap and listened to the argument that ensued. Some of the others seemed to think the Hobble-O was guilty, though Weary stoutly defended the ginger-whiskered, irascible old Shep Taylor. Not once, Chip noticed, did anyone mention Butch Lewis as a possible suspect, nor any of his outfit. Their studied attempt to throw the blame elsewhere made his lip curl. They, couldn't pull that sort of thing on him, he told himself. They must be crazy if they thought all this chewing the rag would make him change his mind about it.

At the time he failed to appreciate their motive as a friendly attempt to ease his feeling of responsibility. At supper he ate in silence, his eyes turned toward his plate. For one thing he had no wish to see J.G.'s face, with its deeper lines of worry, nor did he want to meet his boss's grave, questioning glance. What had passed between them there in the cabin stood out in Chip's consciousness as if all must see the words written in the air. Food choked him. Hungry as he had been, he was the first to push back his plate and straddle backward over the bench at the long table, and he knew that glances followed him when he left the mess house.

In his bunk, with his face turned to the wall and his blankets pulled up over his ears so that only his brown scalp lock was visible, he lay thinking miserably of many things best forgotten. It seemed to him that a curse lay on his life, though why that was so he could not understand. For himself he did not greatly care—or so he said to himself that night. He could take all the hard knocks Fate wanted to hand out to him and take them on his feet. But why must he carry trouble with him to the place that had come to be the only home he knew anywhere in the world? Why must good old J.G. suffer because he had taken in a hoodoo?

Youth touches the heights of exaltation and plumbs the depths of despair. Long after the bunkhouse was dark and silent, save for the snoring of weary young men asleep, Chip Bennett lay motionless under his blankets, every nerve athrob with thoughts too bitter for the boy he was, after all was said. Toward morning he slept, but he did not waken to any brighter mood, he lay in bed until after the others had gone to breakfast.

Then he rose and dressed quickly and busied himself about his bunk. When he went at last to his breakfast, his warbag was packed, his blankets rolled in his bed tarp. The last stragglers joshed him a little and went their way, telling each other that Chip was a damn fool to fight his head over something he couldn't help. And they saddled and went off to comb the range for more saddle horses to throw in the pasture and shape up for spring round-up, planning as they rode how they would handle the beef butchers if they could have their way, and wondering what action J.G. meant to take. They speculated somewhat upon the fact that so far he had not said a word about it, even to Shorty. It was damned queer. They wondered if maybe Chip had lost his nerve after all and didn't tell the Old Man about it.

The trouble was that Chip had not lost his nerve. Jim Whitmore would have felt better if he had. He waited in his cabin, smoking and walking, restless as a caged grizzly, from window to window, pausing at each to look out into the windy, sun-drenched morning. Standing at one window, he saw Chip saddle the blue roan he liked best in his string, and ride away to the upper pasture. Moving uneasily to the opposite window, he watched until Chip came riding back to the corral leading Mike, his own private saddle horse. The others, Jeff the pack horse, Silvia and her two colts, Rummy the irrepressible two-year-old and little Silver the yearling, trotted eagerly behind and around him. They seemed to know that they were going to travel new trails. Their tossing silver manes, the way they lifted rumps at one another in sheer exuberance, told eloquently of their elation.

Jim Whitmore grunted an oath and clamped his teeth down on his pipestem. He turned away from the window—and turned back again, muttering something about a damned young fool. He watched until, saddle changed to Mike's back and the empty pack-saddle cinched gauntly on Jeff, Chip stepped limberly astride Mike and trotted up to the bunkhouse. He waited, smoking furiously in savagely spasmodic puffs, until Chip led his horses up to his door, dropped reins and came in.

J.G. glared at him through a blue cloud. "Bound you'll act the damn fool, ay? Can't take advice from nobody, I s'pose?"

"Not in this case, I can't." Chip looked at him, a swift glance that looked away again. "There's times when a man's got to pick his own trail."

"Man!" J.G. snorted. "Better wait till you're old

enough to vote! Wait till you're dry behind the ears—"

"I'm old enough to tackle any job I know is mine, J.G." Chip spoke gruffly, perhaps to hide how shaken he was. "You wouldn't have much use for a fellow that wouldn't."

Jim Whitmore yanked his pipe from his mouth, glared at it, cursed it for having burned itself out. He turned away to the blanketed table, turned back with his hands outstretched. "Well, here's your pay. Don't go actin' the fool any more'n you have to." He thrust his pipe into his pocket, took it out again, looked at it and thrust it cold between his teeth. "Well, so long. Take care of yourself—and if you—don't be any bigger fool than the good Lord made yuh."

"I'll try not to. Uh—good-bye."

He picked up Mike's reins as if he were in a great hurry to be gone, swung into the saddle and trotted away down along the pasture fence and so out into the old Whoop-up Trail that wound its devious way southward to the river and across to the hills beyond.

IV

HORSES FOR SALE

Barr Lang stood in the doorway of his hotel dining room and eyed the little group of horses clustered around his hitch rail. Across the road at the blacksmith shop, Dave Burch, captain of the Vigilantes—also expert blacksmith between hangings—smoothed his grizzled beard and stared at Chip from under shaggy brows. No doubt he was thinking of the time he came near hanging that young fellow across the way, thinking those same horses had been stolen. Chip thought of it and hated himself for the crimply chill that went up his spine into the roots of his hair, when he saw Burch's cold gaze upon him. For that he walked a little straighter to the door of Lang's store, crowded in between hotel and saloon on the long platform.

Barr Lang came toward him with his fat-throated chuckle. "Well! Looks like you're pullin' your freight! Ain't quittin' the Flying U, are you?"

"Kinda looks that way, don't it?" Then Chip repented of his churlishness. "Yes, I'm heading south again, Mr. Lang. How about a little grub?"

"Sure, sure! Jim'll fix ya up, all right. So you're headin' back down the trail, ay? Colorado, I s'pose?"

Chip forced a grin. "Might, unless I land a job before I get there."

Lang followed him into the store, leaned an elbow on a showcase while Chip found the list he had in his pocket. "Well, now, if you'd of come along yesterday mebby you coulda drawed pay on the trip. Part of the way, anyway. Butch sent a bunch of horses through here. Headin' for Cheyenne. That might of been a chance to work your passage." His little shrewd eyes studied Chip's profile, caught the pinching in of his mouth and drew down his own lip to head off a smile.

"Give me the sugar in a cloth bag, if you can, will you? And if you've got an extra gunny sack for the stuff—" At the clerk's nod, Chip turned and looked full at Lang, meeting the quizzical gleam in his eyes without a sign of understanding.

"I thought Butch was hauling beef this winter," he said carelessly. "What's the matter? Market play out on him?"

Barr Lang's eyes narrowed to slits, then opened their fullest. "Butch? First I heard of it. No, Butch's outfit has been gentlin' saddle horses all winter, far as I know. Got a nice bunch shaped up, from what Hec said. He seen 'em cross the river; said they looked like jim-dandies, every one of 'em." He paused. "The Hobble-O hauled out some beef. Took it out the other way, though. Where'd you hear Butch was sellin' beef?"

"Why, I don't know—somebody said something about it. Might have got things mixed."

"Yeah, I guess they did, all right." Lang gave a good natured chuckle. "Wasn't Butch, I'd bet on that. How's the river today?"

"Don't know," Chip answered. "I patronized the ferry. I wasn't sure just how the ford was, so I didn't try it. Quite a lot of slush ice along the bank."

"Butch forded yesterday, all right," Lang told him. "She won't be high for a month yet, unless they get a chinook up above here, or it comes on to rain. Got your same bunch of horses, I see."

"Yes, same bunch."

"Don't want to sell that mare, do yuh?"

"Not just yet I don't," Chip rebuffed him and paid for his supplies with a gold piece.

Again Lang chuckled. The whole country knew how Chip Bennett felt about those horses of his. He followed Chip to the door and stood on the porch while the sack of provisions was being tied on Jeff. "Well, if you overhaul Butch, mebby he'll give you a job," he called as Chip mounted. "Take care of yourself!"

With lifted hand Chip acknowledged the farewell and rode away from there, scowling thoughtfully at the trail ahead of Mike's nose. Just what had Barr Lang meant to convey? A warning? Or was it just his idea of a joke? He decided that Barr Lang, standing in with everybody as a good hotel-store-saloon keeper must, if he would prosper, merely wanted to let him know that Butch was on the trail ahead of him.

He did not loiter because of that fact. He rode hard, the silver-maned mare and her two colts, fleet as deer, traveling easily where Jeff, the lightly packed bay, puffed and grew gaunt under the pace Chip set, and even the hardy Mike sweated to his ears. Then, miles short of Billings, he turned sharply west in a drizzling rain, and rode to the gate of a snug ranch snuggled back in a coulee, the house hidden among trees.

The front door opened to his knock, lamplight streaming out upon his tall slickered figure and his young face looking old and hard and purposeful. His voice too was metallic with strain.

"Mr. Benton? I'm the fellow who owns the flaxen-maned chestnut mare and colts you wanted to buy in Billings last spring. I've decided to sell. Do you still want them?"

"Why, come in! Come in! I remember you—"

"Thanks, I'm in a hurry. Do you want to buy?"

"Well, if the mare's as good as she was last spring,

and if the colts have shaped up the way they should, I'll buy, yes. Got them with you?"

"They're down by the gate. I want to make Billings before the stores close."

Benton gave him a sharp look. "In trouble, young man?"

Chip's nostrils flared affrontedly. "Nobody's after me," he retorted. "I need money, is all." But for all that, he drove a hard bargain and got his price. But at the last, when he had led up Silver and Rummy and the yearling, his young stoicism broke and he was just a boy seeing his beloved horses taken from him.

His arm went around little Silver's neck, pulling the colt's head close to his breast. "Knock off the price of this colt, Mr. Benton. I'm keeping him. I'll give you a bill of sale for the other two and get going."

With eyes hard as agates—they were so close to tears—and with his heart heavy in his chest, Chip rode away from Benton's ranch. Each lonesome whinny of the colt was like a knife in his chest, and once he stopped and hunted through all his pockets for a lump of cut-loaf sugar, and fed little Silver what solacing crumbs he could find, standing there in the drizzling rain, petting and comforting the orphan until Silver seemed to understand and left off straining at the lead rope and looking back along the trail.

In Billings, with the rain still falling dismally and the streets practically deserted, he left the horses at the livery stable just across from a general store that made a point of remaining open until midnight to accommodate late travelers such as he. Tired though he was, he wrote a short letter to J.G., folded it around the money he had received for the two horses, and got the storekeeper's promise to register and mail it first thing in the morning.

Three trips he made across the street, carrying his purchases into the livery stable office where they would be safe until morning. The last load he carried was a sack of grain for his horses. He went back and looked them over to make sure they were well fed and comfortable, and fed little Silver more sugar from a fresh sack.

Then he hunted a rooming house close by and went to bed, and slept like one drugged until an hour or so before dawn.

At a little all-night lunch place near the depot he ate breakfast, not because he was hungry, but because he wanted to save time and he knew that with his stomach filled now he could ride for half a day without stopping to make camp. He had left orders for the horses to be grained at four o'clock, so they would be ready for the trail by the time he was and would have the heart for a hard day's travel, and now he packed swiftly and dexterously, adding all his supplies to Jeff's load. He was out of town before daylight, just as he had planned.

Two nights later—riding wide of the trail where he could, without losing too much time—he rode down across the willow flat in the teeth of wind and a sleety rain and approached the Missouri. Barr Lang's place showed no glimmer of light, not even in the saloon, which kept late hours. He did not attempt to strike a match and look at his watch, but he knew it must be close to three o'clock in the morning—and this too was as he had planned. Snubbed to its post beside Turk Bowles' squalid shack, the ferry showed its black bulk chuckling at the current, its planks probably a glare of ice.

But he wanted nothing of the ferry that night. With the horses roped together, he urged them into the sullen black water, their hoofs crunching ice at the brink. The next few minutes were a nightmare to Chip. This was the place where his brother Wane had met death in the night; some said by drowning, though Milt Cummings had told Chip it was a bullet from Cash Farley's gun that had sent Wane Bennett down the river. Whatever the cause of Wane's death, Chip always hated the Cow Island crossing, always felt a prickling of the scalp when he must ride into it.

Tonight, with the storm beating in his face and his very bones crying out for rest, the river was a black monster sliding down upon him out of nowhere, pushing against Mike's legs, worrying and clutching, trying to pull him under. In the hissing of the sleet, it seemed that Wane was there beside him, whispering to him that he must not venture upon the trail he meant to ride; urging him back to the Flying U; telling him he had done all he could, selling Rummy and Silvia and sending the money to J.G. Two hundred dollars was quite a lot of money—hardly a drop in the bucket, though, when it was counted against J.G.'s loss. Still, it was all he could do; more than most cowpunchers would think of doing.

With his teeth clamped hard together and his face bowed to the storm, Chip rode doggedly ahead, letting Mike pick his way to suit himself. The horses came out shivering. Tired though they were, he forced them to a lope until the blood ran warm through their chilled bodies, and as they struck into the familiar trail, he could feel the new spring in Mike's stride. Thought he was going home, back to the Flying U. But presently Chip reined him short off the trail, into a long narrow valley leading off toward the Hobble-O and the Lazy Ladder farther down the river.

Neither place drew him, however. He turned again, this time to the left, and entered a brushy draw which opened, a half mile farther on, into a little high-walled basin filled with scrubby timber at its upper end, where a spring creek flowed sluggishly.

Here, in a fair-sized niche in the bluff that gave some shelter from the storm—where a fire, too, would not be seen unless a man rode right up to the place—he made camp, clawing in the dark amongst a thicket for dry wood that would burn. Mike and Jeff, even little Silver, stood close to the fire, snug under blankets Chip pulled from his own bedding. Their contented munching of oats from the feed bags Chip hung over their heads made a pleasant, homey sound within the whistlings of the wind. Their eyes shone green in the reflection of the blaze. When he turned to look at them, Chip saw that they were no longer trembling with cold and weariness.

For himself, he set up the little brown tent bought in Billings. A pup tent, the storekeeper had called it. It was so low that any patch of brush would hide it from view, but it held his bed and his belongings snug from the storm, and when he crawled into it and lay facing the crackling flames, Chip forgot a little of his misery and was almost satisfied with what he had so far accomplished.

There is a content that comes with doing what you have set out to do, however disagreeable the task. When he slept at last, it was his immediate future that had held his last waking thoughts, and not the things he had left behind him.

V

A CLUE IN HAND

DEEP IN THE BADLANDS CHIP LIVED THE LIFE OF THE gray wolves that slunk into the shadows when he rode near. Like the gray wolves he prowled up and down the canyons, though he took the trail at dawn, when the wolves were slinking home from the hunt. Twice he came upon fresh carcasses of beef, too late to catch the killers in the act. For hours at a time he would lie hidden on some high point and watch the country below, using the field glasses he had bought for that purpose in Billings.

On such a day, when he had been nearly a week down there by himself, he lay in a nest between two boulders on a ridge and saw four men ride single file down the gulch beneath him; Weary, Ted Culver, Jack Bates and big, slow-voiced Dick Bird, whom the Flying U boys feared for his sudden rages—but whom they called Dickybird behind his back because the name was so grotesquely inappropriate.

Through his field glasses he watched them lonesomely out of sight, tempted to hail them and hear the sound of a human voice once more. He half rose from his place to shout down to them the chance they were taking of being shot, then settled back again out of sight. They weren't such fools they didn't know all he could tell them about risk. He would be the fool, advertising himself now, after going to all the trouble he had to make his presence in that country a dead secret.

Probably they were down there for the same reason he was—to catch the killers of beef, if they could. They must know that a man cached in the rocks as he was could drop them one by one out of their saddles—like shooting grouse off a pine branch.

Thinking of that, he swung the glasses slowly along the opposite hillside, holding them startled on a wisp of something like smoke drifting across his field of vision. While he watched uneasily, listening for the crack of a rifle, the wisp thickened, widened, until rocks and bushes were completely obscured.

Fog! He lowered the glasses and saw it come flowing into the gulch, reaching with long gray brush strokes to every rock and jutting crag, painting a smooth blankness wherever it touched. He glanced down into the canyon behind him and saw it was the same; and even up where he crouched, the clammy gray was enfolding him. He might have expected it, he thought disgustedly, when the wind died that morning and the air had that muggy, damp feel. Damn such weather, anyway. If he had to waste much more time getting nowhere, the weather would be so warm the damned thieves would have to lay off until fall—unless they were devilish enough to butcher and let the meat rot. They were capable even of that, in his opinion.

Well, the boys would head for home now—and be lucky to make it, if this fog drifted in any worse. And that went for himself, if he didn't slide down off that ridge mighty quick and get back to where he had left Mike. He was inclined now to wish that he had not chosen his camp in the most inaccessible place he could find where a horse could get in and out; a grassy hollow that must have been an old blowhole ages ago, with no outlet except one narrow, twisting fissure between two red hills. The Badlands were full of strange places like that, hard to find even when one knew their location. He hadn't counted on fog.

His horse was tied in a thicket where the grass was too scanty to attract stock and the men he was looking for would not be likely to come. Maybe a mile back of him, the way Chip would have to go, and the sooner he covered that mile the better.

By the time he had reached the foot of the ridge, the gray wall had closed in until he could not see ten feet, and a glance at his watch told him that it was nearly four o'clock in the afternoon—too few hours from darkness to please him much. The sooner he got to camp the better.

He was picking his way carefully along the water-gouged base of the hill, looking for the place where he had climbed up to the grassy slope above the loose red wall of the bank. A tricky place where a fellow could easily sprain an ankle or even break his leg, if he stepped off the edge and took a tumble down that bank. It was considerably farther along where he had started up. He remembered now that he had followed the top of the ridge down quite a long way, keeping under cover as much as possible while he looked for a vantage point with a view into both canyons. He had not come this way where the hill cut straight down, almost as if railroad graders had been at work cutting a level roadbed through.

Damn such a country, anyway. The short grass, curled and matted under the winter storms, was slick as wet soap here, where the slope was steepest. Twice he had to lean and clutch the grass alongside him to keep from going over when his riding boots slipped on fog-jeweled tufts. What he should have done, he now realized, was go back along the top of the ridge to the barren, rocky fold where he had climbed up. But the hill was too steep for that now.

How far he had gone he could not tell with any certainty; half a mile or more, he guessed. The cut bank seemed lower along there, and in places he could almost see the red soil of the canyon floor. Too far down to risk a jump, however, unless he had to do it. So he kept on, edging along with his rifle balanced in his left hand, his right outstretched ready to grab a handful of grass if he felt his feet slipping.

And it was then, while he was sweating over that

precarious footing, that he felt and heard rather than saw something just beneath him. Whether it was an animal or a man, he could not at first determine. He waited, peering over the edge, a growing excitement quickening his pulse so that he felt the blood beating against his temples. Two minutes—three—and a breath of air stirred the gray blanket so that for an instant he saw.

Twenty feet or so down the sheer bank a man was stooping over a carcass lying sprawled on the ground; a beef critter, he knew by the chunky head and wide stubby horns. It was only a glimpse he got, then the fog blanket swung in and blotted the scene.

Chip's teeth snapped together on the oath he had almost shouted. That would have warned the fellow, given him a chance to duck into the fog and get away. And here he was, after almost a week of hunting him, skinning a Flying U critter as bold as you please! If the damned fog would lift again. . . .

He jerked up his rifle, meaning to take aim and wait for another glimpse of the thief. The movement threw him off balance as a treacherous grass turf suddenly gave way under the foot uphill. As he threw his weight instinctively upon the other foot, that slipped as if he had stepped on grease. Flailing wildly with both arms, he fought to recover his balance—and shot over the grassy brink in a sickening plunge.

"What the hell!" The man below yelped as if the words were jarred out of him, when Chip came hurtling down upon him. Had he remained stooping, his back must have been broken by the impact, but he straightened just as Chip landed in a heap on the carcass.

Dazed, the wind knocked out of him and his rifle gone, Chip half rose, groping blindly, clutching for a hold on the thief before the fellow got away. A fist struck him a vicious blow on the side of the head, but his arms went out in a sweeping, grappling motion, got a handful of coat and hung on grimly, as a sharp pain slashed his upper arm and shoulder. He wondered why he couldn't see, then knew that the landing had jammed his hat down over his eyebrows. And he couldn't let go and yank it up out of the way. The fellow struck again, jerked loose and ran.

By the time Chip had gotten to his feet and pulled up his hat, the fog was folded around him in a chill gray wall. Clattering hoofbeats went up the canyon, were presently muffled and lost in the distance.

All he had to show for the encounter were the burning pain across his shoulder, a handful of torn pocket from somebody's coat, a bruised and aching body and a terrible, consuming rage, the greater because humiliation lay beneath it.

VI

FIRST AID FROM POLLY

THE CLIP-CLUP OF A SHOD HORSE TROTTING AMONGST scattered rocks came up the canyon, the sound muffled yet magnified in the fog. Seemed close too. Another damned cow thief, Chip thought, and fumbled for his six-shooter. Shaken, still dazed from his fall and the blow that followed it, he leaned against the red bank and waited grimly, teeth set hard together. There'd be no getaway for this one if he could help it—and he thought he could.

The hoofbeats were almost upon him before he could see the rider, a formless gray shape in the suffocating mass of fog. Chip raised his gun as the hammer clicked back.

"I've got the drop," he announced harshly. "Put up your hands, you blinkety-blink, blank-blank-blank! I'd like nothing better than to fill you so full of lead you'd break your horse's back trying to carry yuh. Pile off, damn yuh, and come over here—and make damned sure you don't crook an elbow while you're getting here."

"Well, of all the gall! You put down that gun and stop your swearing at me, or I'm liable to try a little shooting myself!"

"Huh?" Chip's mouth fell open and hung there in blank amazement.

"You heard me." The rider, a small, slim figure on a chunky brown horse, reined closer. "Don't you try any of your holdup tactics on *me* or you'll wish you hadn't. What do you want, anyway, yelling and bellowing around the way you've been doing?"

Chip found some sort of a voice to use. "And who the devil may you be?" he wanted to know. "If you haven't any more sense than to be down in here, you can't complain at what you may see or hear." His eyes narrowed, blinking a little at the fog which seemed to be creeping into his brain. "What are you, anyhow?

One of these beef butchers?"

The girl kicked her horse, forced it to stand near the fresh carcass and like it. "No, I'm not. And I must say I'm not crazy about your manners. What's going on here, anyway? I thought you were supposed to be headed for Denver."

Chip stared. "Denver? You sure have got the advantage of me—"

"Well," she retorted, "I wouldn't brag about it, if I were you. Last Fourth of July you filled my pitcher with coffee a dozen times, there at the picnic at Cow Island. But of course you didn't see anybody but Julie Lang. You're Chip Bennett and I'm nobody at all—but I would like to know why you're down here, pulling a gun on me and swearing like a trooper at me. I never did anything to you, did I?"

"I—you must be Shep Taylor's girl," Chip muttered confusedly. "I didn't—"

"Well, I'm surprised!" The Taylor girl's tone was elaborately sarcastic. "You actually figured that out! Of course, being introduced to me a couple of times at that darned picnic wouldn't give you the least idea—" She stopped abruptly, drawing in her breath. Her eyes darted here and there, quick glances that saw and registered whatever they fell upon. "What's that blood dripping off your hand for?" she demanded sharply. "I didn't hear any shot. What's been taking place here, anyway? You look," she stated judicially, "sort of as if you'd been sent for and couldn't go."

She swung off her horse like a cowboy and came to him, her gloved hands laying hold of him, lifting his left arm to look at it, turning him a little so that she could see where the blood came from.

"Who slashed you like that?" she demanded fiercely. "You've had a fight, it looks like to me. Was it you that hollered, a few minutes ago?"

"No." Chip's voice was dull, unaccountably listless. "That was the other fellow—yelling when I dropped down the bank on him."

She glanced quickly up the bank, gasped at the height of it, which looked more than it really was, because the top was hidden in the fog. "The fellow that was butchering this beef," she said and looked again at the arm she was holding. "He slashed you with his skinning knife, from the looks of things. I heard a yell and in a minute a horse galloping off up the canyon. Well, we've got to do something about this cut. You're bleeding like a stuck pig, do you know that?"

"I—sure I know it."

His blurred tone made her look at him closely. "Where's your horse? No—wait a minute. We've got to stop this bleeding first thing. Sit down—there on the beef—where I can get at you. You're so tall—"

Chip sat down, leaned his head back against the red bank. Dimly he was aware that the Taylor girl was doing things to his shoulder and upper arm, tearing cloth, wrapping and binding. Funny she should be off down here by herself—no, he remembered now; some of the boys were joshing Weary about Polly Taylor last winter. They said he ought to sling his loop on Polly and take up a ranch. He could run a lot of cattle and never hire help, because Polly was as good as four cowpunchers any day. They said she brought in the strays and held things together. . . . So her being here wasn't so strange, maybe. He began wondering vaguely what she might know about all this.

"That'll have to do till you get where it can be washed out with carbolic," she said. "It's a nasty long slice he took, but it isn't very deep, thank goodness." She was pulling up his shirt collar, his coat. . . . "Lucky for you, old boy, you had on that thick sourdough coat. If you'd been in your shirt sleeves, he'd have just about taken your arm off." She was buttoning him up like a small boy, talking briskly while she worked. "What in the world did you go and jump off that high bank for? It's a wonder you didn't break a leg or something. Why," she asked petulantly, "didn't you shoot him?"

Chip wouldn't tell her then that he fell off the bank. He was afraid she might think that was funny. He didn't see why he had to go weak as a sick cat all at once. It didn't seem as though he had lost enough blood for that. He forgot to consider the shock of that fall added to the knife wound, and it surprised and disgusted him to find himself staggering when he tried to walk. He was like a man drunk.

"What's that you're hanging onto?" Polly Taylor demanded. "Oh. A piece of a coat. I suppose that's your clue," and she smiled unexpectedly up into his face. "Well, keep it, but it probably won't do you much good. Every store in the country sells hand-me-downs of that kind of cloth."

She bullied him into getting on her horse and she insisted upon walking up to where he had left Mike. She wasn't lost, exactly, she declared; she couldn't be, with old Pathfinder there. He'd take her home even in this fog. He'd done it before, when it was dark as a stack of black cats in a cellar. Where was he camped—if it was a fair question? She'd stop by and fix up that cut for him before she went on home.

Chip did not feel much like arguing the point. Sick as he was, lame in every muscle from the fall, he was put to the shameful necessity of riding a girl's horse and letting her walk; though she could have climbed on behind, if she had wanted to. He didn't have much use for girls, anyway. Pretty ones especially. Darned double-crossers, every one of them. This one wasn't pretty—not with those freckles and that red hair in pigtails down her back—but if he let her tag along to camp, she'd go and blab her head off to everyone she saw, telling all she knew about him, and then some. Dressed like a man. Pants and boots, chaps and a man's coat and hat—Chip hated to see a girl trying to ape men. She wore a gun too. He could see why the boys joshed Weary.

Rambling, inconsequential thoughts, but they carried him along through the fog, Polly Taylor leading the horse he rode. She didn't have to, he thought irritably. He was holding the horn just because she had kept the reins herself. He didn't have to be treated like a sick calf, but if she wanted to make herself important around there, let her go to it. He couldn't hunt that fellow in the fog, anyway.

As they neared the thicket where he had left his horse, Mike whinnied to let them know he was there. "Thanks. I'm all right now," Chip said apathetically. "You better go on home. And I wish you'd do me the favor not to say anything about me—"

Polly Taylor stood beside Mike's shoulder, looking up at Chip, watching to see if he were going to fall out of the saddle.

"You'll look nice if you get blood-poisoning in that arm," she told him sharply. "Of course, I won't say anything about you. How big a fool do you think I am? You're down here on the quiet, trying to get the goods on whoever's killing Flying U cattle. Well, what do you suppose I'm here for? You must know they're trying to frame the Hobble-O. We've been filling a beef contract with Fort Assiniboine—"

"Not with hind quarters, I hope?"

"Not on your life. Not any more than belongs to the critter. And we've got the hides to show for every beef we've hauled out." Her chin went up with a sidewise tilt of her head. "We may be hard up, but we haven't come down to peddling any meat but our own. So I'm on a still hunt, same as you. Pa and Snuffle have got their hands full, and the boys have all the chores to do, and we can't afford to hire help except in round-up time."

"A girl's got no business prowling down in here—"

"Why not? I'm no Julie Lang." In that gray half light, her face looked shadowed. "I'm pretty handy with a gun, and that's what all you men bank on for protection, isn't it? And I'd comb hell backwards to help Pa." She glanced around her, an involuntary movement that betrayed her fear. "What I'm afraid of, Mr. Bennett, is that they're trying to frame up a case against him for—the Vigilantes. If they can—"

She broke off abruptly and lifted Chip's rifle to its scabbard. "I picked this up and brought it along. I thought it must be yours," she said and smiled faintly. "And here's something else I found. Belongs to the other fellow, I guess." She swung up into his view a small, blood-stained ax of the kind easily carried behind the cantle, probably wrapped in a gunny sack. A necessary implement, used for splitting down the backbone of a beef and separating the quarters.

"One of the tools of his trade," she said. "You had a taste of the other one. Cheer up, Mr. Bennett. At least, he'll have to hunt himself a new ax."

In his misery Chip took that as a sly dig at his failure to get the man when he had the chance. Had the fellow right there within reach and this was all he had to show for it! Even lost his rifle—and of course it had to be the girl who found it and brought it along—and then gave it back to him with that sarcastic smile on her face. Hell, she was treating him like a tenderfoot!

He came near refusing to tell her where his camp was, but that knife cut was throbbing and burning so badly he thought maybe she was right about blood-poisoning and he had better let her fix it up; it was in such a darned awkward place he couldn't attend to it himself; on the point of his shoulder and running down the back of his arm, like that, he'd have to be a contortionist to get at it. And he cursed the luck that made him need the girl's help.

He resented too the fact that she was not impressed with his hideout. Oh, yes, she said, she knew about that little basin. The Devil's Dipper, she called it, because of its shape. She didn't know how many knew about it; not many, she guessed. It would do for the present, though the spring in there always dried up along in July, and it was the worst place for snakes she'd ever seen. Safe enough now, though. But if he wanted a real hideout, she'd show him one that certainly was a dandy. Folks could hunt till they were blind and they'd never find it.

All this when they had wormed their way into the Devil's Dipper. Outside, she hadn't talked more than was absolutely necessary, because you couldn't tell how close someone might be in the fog and it didn't pay to take a chance.

Chip resented her shrewdness. And he hated the unconcerned efficiency she displayed in getting a fire started, boiling water and a flour sack he'd swear was clean as soap and water could make it; boiled a needleful of white thread too, and dried it by the fire, while she washed the cut with carbolic water so hot he could scarcely keep from yelling when it touched the raw flesh. She was very efficient too, in sewing up the wound. At least, he judged she was, she hurt so damnably, sewing over and over and taking as many stitches as she thought were needed, with no apology for the pain.

She had Chip sweating and gritting his teeth with the agony of her ministrations, but all he said was,

"I'll bet you're a dandy at doctoring horses." His tone left no doubt whatever of his meaning.

Polly Taylor calmly buttoned his collar and tied another flour sack around his neck for a sling. "Yes. When Pathfinder got cut up in our new barb-wire fence, you should have seen the sewing I had to do. He looked like a crazy quilt when I got through, and he kicked three boards off the stable. But he sure healed up nice."

Darn her, she didn't even crack a smile to show whether she meant it or not.

He had to admit, though, that he felt better after the first pain was over, and that the supper she cooked was the best meal he had eaten since Billings; which was surprising, since Chip privately considered himself the best camp-fire cook in the country. He had also a reluctant appreciation of the way she washed the dishes and tidied camp afterwards, but that did not mean he liked her any better.

He was glad when she finally led up her horse, stuck a very small boot toe into the stirrup and went up with a springy lightness into the saddle. Thanks he gave her, as his mother had taught him to do. She dismissed them with a shrug and a wave of her hand, oddly out of keeping with her role as a simple ranch girl.

"The unwritten law of the range," she said, with an arresting irony in her voice. "Lie around camp and don't try to use that arm, and don't monkey with the bandage, either. I'll be back in a couple of days to take a look at it."

"Don't put yourself out on my account," Chip hoped that didn't sound like a snub, but he didn't want her fussing around him, and that was the truth. "And don't get lost," he added perfunctorily.

"Oh, Pathfinder will take care of that, all right," she said carelessly, and gave him a long studying glance as she swung her horse out into the smothery blackness of the night.

Well, she was good-hearted, all right, but he was glad she was gone. He must have been. He told himself so at least a dozen times before he slept.

VII

WHY WAIT FOR PROOF?

THE NEXT DAY SNAILED BY, A SODDEN CENTURY between dripping dawn and a drizzling dusk. Chip remained within the Devil's Dipper and would have slept the hours away, if his arm had let him. Since its throbbing kept him awake, he did plenty of thinking. The result of his meditations slipped out while Polly Taylor was talking next day about the stealing. He hadn't intended to discuss the matter—or any other—with Polly, but somehow he found himself telling her all about the trouble with Cash Farley and the rest of Big Butch's gang, and just why he had taken it upon himself to run them down on rustling.

Polly hadn't thought about Butch Lewis as the guilty party. She was sure that it was an attempt to implicate the Hobble-O and Butch had always been a pretty good neighbor. "Anyway, he doesn't pay any attention to cattle," she argued. "What he goes after is horses."

The same old argument. It made Chip tired. "He goes after whatever will put the biggest crimp in the other fellow," he stated. "He's after the Flying U because I'm working there; or was. I've got to catch him pretty quick, now, or the weather'll be too warm to haul out more beef. He must take it out the other way, toward Glasgow. He'll have to lay off pretty soon now, so I'm going to get busy."

"Not with that arm," Polly told him flatly. "And they're not selling the beef. They don't care how warm the weather gets; they'll go on killing whenever they find a critter handy. It isn't any selling proposition at all."

"No?"

"Why, no! Haven't you caught on yet?" Polly sweetened the dried apples and set them aside to cool. Her cheeks were red from bending over the fire, almost as red as her mouth, Chip noticed. All the short hairs curled in little ringlets around her face. . . . If she had a mind to fix herself up a little, she'd be good-looking—not that it mattered.

"Caught on to what?" he asked guardedly, knowing beforehand it was just some silly girl notion of hers.

"Why, the—the devilish meanness of them. The foxy way they're keeping clear and making it look like Papa's work. They aren't selling any beef. All they do is skin out the hind quarters and pack them off somewhere and dump them. I can show you one place where they threw at least a dozen into a ravine."

"You sure of that?"

"Of course." She gave him a quick, impatient glance. "Didn't I just say I saw a whole pile of them?" She stood up to go and suddenly rage took hold of her. Both her small hands doubled into fists. "Killing's too good for a man that will do such a thing! I'll pin it on him before I'm through—"

"*You* will!" Chip's snort of amused contempt was maddening. It placed her down where children strut and brag. "I expect to handle this situation myself," he added, with a tightening of the mouth. "It's a little outside a woman's province, I'm afraid."

"Oh, yes, you'll handle it!" Polly Taylor looked furious. "If it's left for *you* to handle— You'd let them make a case against the Hobble-O that would cost my father his life! That Cow Island bunch is just waiting for a chance—"

"Calm yourself," was Chip's ironical advice. "Your father has nothing to do with this. I'm the one they're after, and I'm going to Butch Lewis and call for a show-down right now!" Though his voice was calm enough, Chip's eyes and the flare of his nostrils betrayed how angry he was. "I'll thank you not to meddle in this affair."

"Oh, *will* you!" Polly's breath was coming fast. "You must think you're some punkins, having Butch Lewis and his bunch spending their time killing Flying U cattle just because they're mad at you! Let me tell you one thing, Chip Bennett: If Big Butch was after you, he'd *get* you! Don't make any mistake about that. He certainly wouldn't take out his spite killing beef—he'd hunt you up and put a bullet through you, and no ifs or ands about it!"

"Yes?"

"Yes!" stormed Polly. "And you needn't speak to me in that supercilious tone of voice, either. You're so darned conceited you think you've started a range war, just because you got Butch Lewis down on you!" She snatched up her gloves, buttoned herself into her coat with indignant haste, and with an angry toss of her head, she went over to her horse and mounted him like a boy who was so mad he couldn't see straight.

But she could not resist a last fling at Chip. She reined over to the fire and looked at him stormily. "If you ever should accidentally find out the truth of this matter," she said, in a suppressed tone of bitterness, "I'm afraid you're going to get the worst jolt you've ever had. You'll find out you don't figure in it at all. And you needn't waste your time on Butch Lewis, I can tell you that much."

Chip permitted his mouth a scornful twist at one corner. "Sorry if he's a particular friend of yours, Miss Taylor—"

"Oh, you—"

"Because I'm certainly going after him."

Miss Taylor gave another toss of her head. "Yes, I've got a picture of you going after Big Butch!" And with that she kicked Pathfinder with her spurs and hurtled off toward the crevice before Chip could translate his emotions into language permissible in the presence of a lady.

"Damn it, I wish she'd been a man when she said

that," he gritted helplessly, glaring after her. And he began to pack his belongings—with one hand mostly—and left the Devil's Dipper with his mind wrathfully fixed upon following his own trail regardless. He had talked pretty big about going after Big Butch and calling for a show-down; he wasn't quite ready to commit suicide, he told himself grimly; he'd have to wait for some proof before he did anything quite so drastic as that. But he also told himself that he'd be damned if he were going to let Polly Taylor or any other girl lead him around by the nose. He wasn't broken to lead, he'd have her know.

That day he spent in finding another camp where that darned Taylor girl couldn't locate him. It wasn't easy. He was obliged to go deeper into the Badlands, where few cattle had been tempted to stray, and where the beef butchers would not bother to look for them, their object being to kill beef where they would be found.

The camp he chose didn't suit him, and by night he was so mad at Polly Taylor and so miserable with his arm and certain bruised areas that began to raise cain with him after hours in the saddle, that he was ripe for any crazy notion that seized him. And in the night one came and found him awake and eager to receive it.

Why wait for proof? Didn't he know enough already—all he needed to know? The brilliance of that short cut of logic dazzled him so that he could hardly wait for daylight. It never occurred to him that a touch of fever was behind the brilliance.

A light snow had fallen in the night. Fine weather

for trailing the beef killers, he thought; but he wasn't going to monkey around any longer hunting them.

"When you want to kill a snake, you don't start in on his tail," he muttered. "You go to work on his head, by thunder." Which he immediately proceeded to do, breaking camp again and taking the pack horse and colt along with him. The particular snake he was after holed up in a canyon he did not know, but he did know one end of the trail that led to it, and rather than spend hours of haphazard searching in that wild and broken country, he headed toward the Whoop-up Trail.

Where three canyons branched like spread fingers, Chip took the one farthest to the left—a turning that had nearly spelled disaster for him last summer, when he had three outlaws in tow and the horse he rode had known this trail all too well. That ride had been in moonlight, and now the shadowless gray light gave an altogether different aspect to the narrow winding gulch he followed. But certain little landmarks there was no mistaking and Chip's memory held like glue any trail he had once ridden over. He made the right turnings into several different gulches and canyons and so came out finally into the one he wanted. If he had had any doubt of that, two sets of fresh horse tracks pointed the way before him. He followed them boldly, still pleased with his idea.

He came out into a basin which on a map must have looked like the fat body of a tarantula, it was so surrounded by crooked legs of canyons and ravines. At one side, where a willow-fringed creek flowed through, he glimpsed a crude rail fence through the trees, but the hoofmarks led straight on through the snow to where the hills came down in a notch filled with juniper and pines. The end of the trail, by the look of things. He loosened the gun in his holster and rode forward, grim and watchful as a wolf.

VIII
BIG BUTCH

SEVERAL HORSES LOAFED IN A ROUND-POLE CORRAL, and three of them carried sweaty saddle marks and had been hard ridden, by the look of them. Behind the corral a log stable squatted against the brush-fringed wall of the basin, and farther along, half concealed within the thicket, huddled a log cabin larger than the average size favored by bachelor outfits. Chip found the trail of boot tracks in the snow and followed.

He had no special plan, except that he was going to face Butch Lewis and call for a show-down. After that—well, he didn't much care what came after that, so long as he put a stop to the depredations against the Flying U. They might kill him, but he'd go down fighting, anyway.

In that crazy mood he dismounted stiffly before the cabin and limped to the door. With his good hand, he rapped peremptorily upon the stout planking.

"Come in!" two voices bellowed in chorus, and Chip pushed open the door and stepped inside.

Silence greeted him. After hours of looking at snow, the room seemed to him black dark, but he knew that he stood sharply revealed to others who were watching him. He could feel their eyes upon him, probing for his errand there; could feel too how fingers caressed triggers, waiting for his first hostile move.

"Is Butch Lewis here?" Even though he could not see a thing, Chip's glance moved around the room.

Chip leaned his back against it, a little scared now at his foolhardiness in coming here like this. It did not show in his face, however, nor in his manner, which was stony calm. As his eyes adjusted themselves to the half light, objects revealed themselves, vaguely at first, then with sharper details. Four men sat around a table smoking, the remains of a meal before them. All were eyeing him distrustfully, their right hands hidden—holding guns, he knew well enough without being told. He waited.

"Well, what do you want of me? Who in hell are yuh, anyway?"

That was Big Butch, then. Chip had not been sure. Butch was sitting facing him, eyeing him curiously, with his hands out of sight.

"I guess you knew Wane Bennett—heard of him at least. I'm his brother Chip, that took Wane's horse away from Cash Farley last Fourth of July. I also rounded up Cash and a couple more of your men and turned them over to Dave Burch for horse thieves. I'm the man they tried to kill last summer, over toward One Man Coulee—the time Cash Farley and three of your men were shot."

"Yeah? And what you braggin' about it now for?"

Chip eased his sore arm in its sling, his eyes never

leaving Butch's face. "I'm not bragging. I'm just laying my cards on the table and calling for a showdown. I'm off the Flying U payroll now—quit them almost two weeks ago—"

Big Butch eyed him curiously. "What the hell difference does that make?"

"Well, damn it, I'm the one you've got it in for. Not the Flying U. J.G. never did a thing to you in his life. You've been taking out your grudge on him and you've got to quit it. I'm willing to fight it out alone. Leave the Flying U strictly out of it. Do your Injun act with me. But I'll tell you right now, Cash Farley asked for all he got and so did those others."

Big Butch darted a sidelong glance at one of the men, who immediately rose and hitched up his pants, as if he were getting himself ready for action, though all he did was sidle over toward Chip and wait for further orders. Butch's light blue eyes showed in gleaming slits between his blonde lashes.

"Who all's with yuh?"

"Nobody. I don't ask anyone to fight my battles for me."

"Sam, you go take a look around."

A lean dark man got up and disappeared through a dark doorway in the far corner of the room, his sliding gait somehow like a coyote's. Butch waited, his blank speculative stare never leaving Chip's face.

Then Sam slipped in the back way, puzzled creases between his black eyebrows. "He come alone, Butch, far as the canyon, anyway. Got a pack horse and a yearlin' colt out front here, beside his saddle horse.

Looks like he's moved in."

Butch grunted something under his breath. "Might be a blind, at that. You and Flicker go take a look back in the canyon. Don't show up here till you're dead sure nobody's trailin' him. Anybody you run acrost, bring 'em in. Sime, you better go along." He brought a hand up in sight, laying his gun on the table. Its muzzle stared like a round black eye at Chip.

"Come and set down, feller. Sam, pour him some coffee before yuh go." With his left hand, Butch smoothed down his reddish mustache, his watchful gaze still on Chip. "Seddown, I told yuh! You're just as easy to kill settin' down as you are standin' up, ain't you? You and me has got some chin whackin' to do here."

He waited until Chip decided to sit down at the table, his hat on the floor beside him. He watched while Chip deliberately drew his gun, laid it on the table beside him.

"Maybe you'd just as soon not shoot a man that hasn't got a chance," Chip said matter of factly, as if he did not know that at least one of the three had stopped at the back door and was watching every move he made. "Your gun's cocked. Mine isn't. If you call that an even break—"

"Hell, you're crazy as a loon," said Butch and grinned. He turned his gun aside, let down the hammer with his thumb. "That, or you've got the nerve of a brass monkey. I ain't goin' to shoot yuh, kid; not unless you crowd me into it. Drink your coffee and eat a little something. You look like you needed it."

The door behind Chip clicked shut. The two were alone together in the cabin. "Well," Chip said harshly, "what are you going to do about it? Are you going to let the Flying U alone—quit butchering their beef—or what?"

Butch passed a dish of fried venison, setting it down within easy reach, when Chip made no move to take it. "So that's what's eatin' on yuh? Beef rustlin', huh?" He pursed his lips, his mustache ends standing straight out. "You think I been doin' all that butcherin'? That why you rode in here, just to bone me about it?"

"What else?" Chip's glance bored into Butch's light eyes. "To make you fight in the open. If you've got it in for me—"

"Hell's fire, kid!" swore Butch. "Any little trouble you might of had with Cash, it was him and you for it. You never heard me make any complaint, did you? Matter uh fact, you done me a favor and didn't know it. Cash was gittin' too big for his boots around here. Pullin' some of the boys over to him. Why," Butch confided earnestly, "damn it, kid, I never had a thing to do with it that time they run off them Flyin' U horses last summer. That was Cash, branchin' out fer himself. It was him wanted to git you for draggin' him into Cow Island. Why, hell, I'd sent that bunch off the other way to see about gittin' delivery on some horses I bought. I never knowed they was over swappin' lead with you boys till it was all over."

"According to you, then, you're plumb overflowing

with gratitude to me. Is that the idea?" Chip's voice dripped sarcasm.

"Wel-l, I ain't hos-tyle any," drawled Butch, laugh wrinkles showing around his eyes. "You done me a favor last summer, whether you knowed it or not. Me and Cash was about due to lock horns over who was boss around here. All them boys you folks beefed over your way, they was troublemakers from the word go." He slid the bean dish invitingly toward Chip. "No, I ain't got it in for yuh, kid. You saved me some trouble, maybe."

"Then if that's the case," Chip retorted, "what's your object in butcherin' Flying U cattle and letting half of 'em lay and rot? If that ain't spite work, what is it? Even a coyote has his own reasons for pulling down calves."

Dull crimson flowed up to roots of Butch's sandy hair. "Go easy there on the name callin'," he warned. "Where'd you git the idea't I'm back of that beef rustlin'? Hell, I ain't no beef peddler—and skinnin' cattle on a cold day ain't my idea of fun."

It was Chip's turn to grow red. "Well, after all that trouble last summer with your outfit, a fellow 'd naturally suppose—" He broke off. He hadn't a scrap of real evidence against Butch. He was just guessing; had been all along. "No one else has any grudge against the Flying U," he finished lamely.

"Say!" cried Butch hotly. "When I git a grudge agin a man, he knows it right now! Him and his fond relations, when they send out for the body." He leaned angrily across his dirty plate, his pale blue eyes like polished steel. "If I had a grudge agin you or the outfit you work for—damn it, I'd be bouncin' bullets offn your damn' carcass long ago. I sure wouldn't go around skinnin' cattle to git even. That's a cinch."

Chip eyed him doubtfully, convinced in spite of himself. He chewed a corner of his lip, laid a hand on his sore arm, aware now of its throbbing, which in the heat of his accusations he had not noticed.

"Well, maybe I've been barking up the wrong tree," he said wearily. "But if you aren't at the bottom of it, who is?"

Butch stared him down. "You know who's been haulin' out beef by the four-horse loads all winter," he said finally. "Or don't yuh?"

"The Hobble-O, you mean? I don't believe—"

"Suit yourself," Butch said gruffly. "If old Shep can git away with it, that's all right with me. I ain't buyin' in on what's none of my business."

"But they've got hides to show for all the beef—"

"Yeah? That's fine. All their beef contracts with the fort, I s'pose—and all the hind quarters they peddle between here and there!" Butch laughed a little.

Chip gave him a quick, sharp look. "Have they been peddling hind quarters along the road? Do you know that for a fact?"

Butch settled back in his chair, chuckling to himself. On a sudden impulse he leaned further, twisted his huge body and with a long arm reached the coffeepot steaming on the stove. He filled his cup, held the pot toward Chip.

"Lemme pour yuh some hot coffee," he said. "It

ain't goin' to poison yuh to eat outlaw grub, as they call it. You keep your business under your own hat in this country and you git the name of bein' an outlaw. Cash and some of the boys kinda got it into their heads they oughta live up to it, looks like. Served 'em damn right. Kid, you look sick. What happened to your arm?" His voice changed, was gruffly friendly and sympathetic. Casting a glance around the table, he picked up a clean tin cup, filled it and held it out to Chip. "You and me oughta git along fine," he grinned. "You sure have got nerve—comin' here and jumpin' me about that beef killin', like you had a regiment uh soldiers behind your back. By—I'll put in any time with a man that's got guts!"

Chip was human enough to soften a little to that friendly attitude. He took the cup and drank the strong hot brew thirstily, but over the rim his brown eyes still held their look of purpose that would not be turned aside.

"Just what do you know about the Hobble-O peddling hindquarters—?"

"Say!" Butch's tone was a direct protest. "I don't want to git mixed up in this, kid. Me and the Hobble-O has been gittin' along just fine, leavin' each other strictly alone. Shep's got women folks and a couple of kids to feed. I wouldn't want to git him into no trouble."

"But that remark you made; that's straight goods, is it?"

Butch spooned more sugar into his coffee. "That they've been peddling on the side? Sure, it is. I know of several places where they sold a hind quarter on the way up to the fort. Course, you can't tell by the color of the meat what brand it wore." He grinned. "I don't know—Flyin' U beef tastes about the same as Hobble-O, I reckon."

"Somebody might be trying to frame the Hobble-O." When Polly Taylor had said that, Chip had thought it silly. It looked more plausible now.

Butch gave a snort of dissent. "Who? The Flyin' U, maybe? It sure as hell ain't me. I got my work cut out, mindin' my own business and livin' down the lies folks peddle about me."

Chip watched Butch refill his cup with coffee, said "Whoa" at the proper time and drank it straight down. "Well, looks like I've strayed into a box canyon on this rustling business," he said gloomily. "I was so dead certain it was you, Butch, I never looked for anybody else. I sure would like to know who it was I jumped the other day in the fog."

He proceeded to tell exactly how that encounter had come about, watching Butch's face while he talked. Butch was interested, but it was perfectly apparent that he was hearing it for the first time. And he had no idea who might have slashed Chip; or said he had none. But he asked how far it was from the Hobble-O, and he looked slightly amused when Chip told how the girl had come along just then and had sewn up the wound for him.

"And uh course you swallowed all she told yuh," Butch commented.

"Well, not—"

He did not finish the sentence. The door was pushed open and someone was propelled into the room, the man Sime following immediately after.

Butch stared in astonishment, and with his cup poised halfway to his mouth, Chip turned to look at the newcomer.

It was Polly Taylor. Her hat was knocked aslant on her head, a lock of hair had fallen down across her forehead and across one blazing eye. From shoulders to hips a rope was wound around and around her slim body, pinioning her arms to her sides.

IX
POLLY BUYS IN

THE BOX CHIP WAS SITTING ON TURNED OVER WITH A bump as he sprang up, reaching for his gun on the table. A purely instinctive action born of his impulse to rescue the girl, Polly chose to put a different interpretation upon it!

"So you're in on this too!" she flung at him. "You didn't come here to fight Butch—you just decided to move in out of the weather. And I, like a fool, thought you were going to need protection! Made it in time for dinner, I see." Her voice was high, strident with impotent fury. "Well, go ahead, why don't you? Shoot me for finding out what a liar you are!"

"I wouldn't be any bigger a fool than the Lord made me, if I were you," Chip advised her bitingly. "I certainly didn't give you the impression I needed a woman's protection, I hope!"

Butch was on his feet, brushing past Chip. "What did you bring that girl here for?" he demanded harshly of Sime, his glance going past him to Sam and Flicker, who had come in and were standing by the door, uncertain of the next move. "Take that damned rope off her, you chump!"

"She's a hell-cat, Butch," Sime demurred. "We trailed her up among the rocks, where she was watchin' camp with a rifle. Had her glove off all ready to shoot when me and Flicker nabbed her—and lookit what she done to me!" He displayed scratches on his face, one close to the corner of his eyes and another deep one raked down the side of his high nose. "Tried to claw m' eyes out. We brung her in, like you said, but we shore had one hell of a time till we roped her. You better leave it stay right where it's at, Butch—"

"Who the hell's runnin' this camp? You or me?" And as Sime flung up his hands in a gesture of dismissal, throwing all responsibility on the boss, Butch untied the rope and flipped it off the girl. But his eyes had not softened in the slightest degree.

"What are you doing down in here, anyway?"

Polly Taylor twitched her shoulders as the rope left them, tucked back the lock of hair and pulled her hat straight, while Butch eyed her.

"That's none of your business, that I can see. You make that cutthroat of a Flicker give me back my guns and be quick about it too!"

"What was you spyin' on this camp for? You know what happens to spies, don'tcha?" Butch scowled down at her with the fearsome air of a man trying to scare a child into good behavior.

"Fiddlesticks!" snapped Polly. "You're not going to do a thing and you know it as well as I do. You wouldn't dare." Her glance swung contemptuously to Chip. "I did think I might be needed here. But I guess not. You don't seem to be in any great danger, after all."

"If I were," Chip snapped back at her, "I certainly wouldn't holler to you for help. It seems to me you're taking a good deal upon yourself, Miss Taylor, when you follow me around with the mistaken idea of taking care of me."

"I sure was a fool for believing a word you said," she cried. "Pretending you had it in for Butch and all the time—"

"Why," Big Butch cut in, "me and Chip's the best of friends. I was just offerin' him a job breakin' horses." He looked at Chip.

Polly gasped. "Why—is that—would you go to work for Butch Lewis?"

Her tone was so shocked, so incredulous, that Chip's pride was stung to a cold fury. "And why not, if I took the notion?" His tone asked further if it were any business of hers what he did. It was as if there were two of him standing there, looking at the girl, and as if one of him were furious because the rest of him was touched by her concern for his welfare; touched and sorry for the humiliation she would die rather than admit. But the furious one was the stronger one just now and did all the talking, because he was young enough to be terribly afraid these men might think he was under a woman's thumb; tied to this girl's apron string. His face and voice chilled. "Busting broncs is my line of work," he added, not looking at her.

Polly gave him a withering stare. "Yes, you certainly are in fine shape to bust broncs," she reminded him. "It's nothing to me, of course—but I was under the impression you had another job staked out for yourself. I see I was wrong. It's worth the trip down here to get the facts."

"You've got no call to be down here," Butch said severely. "Your folks oughta keep you to home. Taggin' a feller around the country—it ain't purty. You'd better be home helpin' your maw."

"T-tagging a fellow around—" Rage choked Polly Taylor. "Oh, I could kill the whole bunch of you!"

From the corner of his eye Chip stole a glance at her, saw her swallow with clenched teeth, her eyes blinking back the tears. In spite of his affronted pride, in spite of those four scowling men eyeing her, he had a strong impulse to put an arm around her straight little shoulders and comfort her somehow. It was a damned shame. Butch and all of them rowing with her like that. She meant all right. . . .

"Give me my guns, Butch Lewis!"

Butch grinned. "What for? To shoot me with? Not on your life." He looked at her, twisting his mustache. From under his eyebrows he shot a glance at his men. "Sam and Flicker, you go with her as far as the Hobble-O line fence—"

"They shall not! I won't have them near me!"

"—and give her back her guns when she's on her

own land; or her paw's land, rather." He picked up her rifle, pumped out all the shells, picked them off the floor and handed them gravely to Polly. He motioned to Sime for her six-shooter, took it and emptied the cylinder before he gave the two guns to Sam.

"Good-bye, Miss Taylor; sorry you can't stay longer," he said, with a sardonic smile. "The boys'll see yuh safe home. And if you'll take a fool's advice, you'll stay there after this and keep your nose out of other folks' business."

Chip made an impatient movement, looked past Polly at the three men. Evidently they did not impress him, for he turned to Butch and said, "I'll see that she gets home all right." He stooped for his hat.

"No need of your going, Chip. She'll get home all right—or I'll know the reason why." He sent a glance toward his men that made them stir uneasily and look away.

"That isn't the point, Butch," Chip said curtly. "She doesn't want to go with them. That's reason enough, I should think."

Polly threw up her chin—a mannerism he knew well. "Oh, if it comes to that," she declared, "I'll choose the least of two evils. I'll go with Sam and Flicker." And without a glance toward Chip, she turned and walked to the door, opened it with a jerk and paused to say over her shoulder, "There's another day coming; just remember that!" and went out with that defiant upward tilt of her head.

Sam and Flicker started to follow. Butch's voice overtook them in the doorway. "You two make sure that girl gits home all right—and watch your dodgers, or I'll hang your hides on the fence."

Without a word they went out. Butch rolled himself a cigarette, his face thoughtful. Sime picked up the water bucket from the bench beside the door and disappeared, going to the spring. Over the match blaze as he lighted his cigarette, Butch studied Chip's face set in inscrutable calm.

"Sharp as they make 'em, that Taylor girl," he drawled, after a puff or two. "Been out all winter scoutin' for her dad. Couldn't a jackrabbit move an ear within a mile that she wouldn't know." He drew at his cigarette, savoring the smoke. "Wish I knowed what she really was after, down here. Trailin' you, maybe—suspicious as hell. You don't want to swallow all she hands yuh, kid."

Chip did not speak. He was thinking, maybe that accounted for Polly Taylor being so close when he fell on that rustler. Maybe it *was* her dad, or Snuffle Jones, and maybe that was why she stuck beside him, found out where he camped, kept in touch afterwards. Maybe she knew that ax she picked up. Hell, was there anyone a fellow could trust?

Butch sauntered to the bunk, sat down and leaned back at ease against a roll of blankets. Left his gun on the table, which no outlaw would be likely to do. Chip wondered at that, wondered too if people didn't have a wrong impression of Lewis.

Sime came in, set the sloshing bucket on the bench. Butch yawned loudly. "How's the weather, Sime?" he called in a lazy tone of well fed comfort.

“Fixin’ to storm again. Wind’s switched to the northwest. She’ll be blizzardin’ before mornin’, I reckon.” Sime dipped water into a dishpan, refilled the stove with wood and set the pan on to heat.

“Better go show the kid here where to put his horse. He can unpack and throw his stuff in here. His horses’ll stand in the stable tonight.” Butch sat up. “No, I’ll go myself.” He got up, went over and picked up his gun. “Come on, Chip. Might as well gentle down to the fact that you’re here to stay a while.”

Threat or invitation, Chip could not tell. “Suits me,” he said briefly and went out ahead of Butch.

One thing was certain. Before he left that basin, he meant to know to his own satisfaction whether Butch Lewis were a much maligned man, blamed for the deeds of such men as Cash Farley had been, or whether he merited the name of outlaw. At that moment Chip did not know what to think. While Butch stuck beside him, helping him put his horses in the stable, casually friendly talk lightening the task, Chip watched for some hint, some sign that would give him a clue to his real status with Big Butch Lewis. He watched in vain. Prisoner or welcome guest—to save his life, he could not tell which name he might apply to himself.

And that was something he meant to find out.

X

MILT MAKES HIS TALK

WITH SHRIEKING FURY OF WIND, THE POWDERY SNOW drove across the high ranges. Before it the cattle drifted miserably mile after mile, with heads bent and swinging in rhythm with each plodding step they took. Hunting shelter, they left the benches and sought the deepest coulees and creek bottoms, where they huddled close together in the bushes. The snow, fine as flour packed in the hair, made hard, little ridgy drifts along their backs. Standing so, while the blizzard lasted, they ate the twigs with buds all frozen, and were hungry still.

Three days that blizzard lasted, and the leanest cows died standing in the drifts that packed certain low places. Through other days and nights the cold wind blew from out the north, packing the snow deep in every crease and hollow. By then it was April and the early calves shivered on their bandy legs and only the toughest survived; which meant a poor calf crop that year, in spite of all the good weather to follow.

Jim Whitmore rode grimly out with his men to see what toll the storm had taken and to judge for himself what damage the beef rustlers had done to his fall shipments. He saw enough to set him glowering in his cabin at night, his tough old jaws clamped hard upon his pipe, while he meditated upon protective measures—yes, and upon reprisals as well. Though all he could do now would not bring back his slaughtered steers nor lessen the ravages of the big March storm upon his cows and calves.

He was thinking about it one Sunday afternoon—the first pleasant Sunday since the blizzard—when Weary, jingling his spurs, walked up the path from the corral and put his head into J.G.'s open doorway.

"Couple of riders coming up the creek," he announced in his pleasant drawl. "Milt Cummings' paint pony that he rides on Sundays—and I think it's Spike Reilly with him." He paused, his head turning for further inspection of the approaching horsemen. "Yep, it's them, all right. I just thought I'd tell yuh, J.G., in case you didn't happen to be in the mood for company."

J.G. hadn't been in the mood for anything except a fight lately, and he proved it now by jerking his pipe from his worried-looking mouth and swearing querulously at Weary. "And what call has anyone on this ranch got to think I ain't in the mood fer any dawgoned thing that comes along?" he finished—though not so mildly as it is set down here. "You tell Milt Cummin's I want to see him. By this and by that, there's a few questions I want to ask—"

Weary, however, was gone out of hearing, walking fast to the corral. He needn't have hurried so much. Milt Cummings halted only long enough to say hello to what boys were in sight and to ask where he would find their boss. He and Spike met Weary in the path and rode on with a curt greeting.

Weary kept on to where he found an audience. "Mamma! The Old Man sure is fighty today," he reported, in a tone of concern. "Damn near blowed me outa my boots when I asked him was he in the mood for company. Milt's liable to be huntin' a high fence if he ain't careful; kinda looked like he was on the prod himself about something, didn't yuh think?"

"Sure has got something on his chest," Shorty agreed. "Maybe I better go along up there and see what he wants."

Weary grinned widely. "Better ride your runnin' horse then. You're liable to need him."

Up at the boss's cabin, Milt Cummings was off his horse and squatted on his boot heels beside the doorway where J.G. sat sucking at his pipe. Beside Milt his top hand, Spike Reilly, leaned against the log wall and built himself a cigarette with a noncommittal air of detachment from the conversation.

Cigarette between the fingers of his left hand, Milt picked up a dried-weed stalk and was absently drawing meaningless patterns on the hard-trodden earth. He looked up at J.G. and the sun brought out a greenish tint in his gray eyes.

"J.G., I've been losing a hell of a lot of cattle, the last six months," he said abruptly.

J.G. grunted, took his pipe from his mouth and spat out to one side of the doorway. "Got it figured out how a Lazy Ladder can be worked over into a Flying U, Milt?"

Milt made a disclaiming gesture with the cigarette hand. "You know damn well I ain't. I've been wondering if maybe—mine's been butchered," he explained. "I've been wondering if maybe you've lost some that way."

"Some."

"Any idea who's been doing it?" Milt's green-gray eyes swung a glance to Jim Whitmore's face, hung there, keenly watchful.

"No proof, so fur." Weary would have been astonished at J.G.'s calm and at the placid, unrevealing mask of his lined and leathery countenance.

"You know, I s'pose, the Hobble-O's been hauling out beef all winter?"

"I know that; sure. And there's quite a few Hobble-O cattle runnin' the range. I know that too." J.G. crowded the charred tobacco down into his pipe. "S'picion ain't proof, Milt. Taylor's got a right to sell his own beef and sell it any way he's a mind to."

Milt flung away the weed with a quick, angry motion. "Well, by gosh, he's got no right to kill mine and sell it! Uh course, if you're a mind to donate a carload of good beef to his cause, that's your own lookout. No skin off my nose if he beefs every critter you've got to your name. But me, I ain't built that way."

J.G. took three hard, slow pulls at his pipe. "You got any proof, Milt, that it was them done it?"

"Proof?" Milt snorted. "Spike, have we got any proof?" Glance and tone were ironic.

"Proof enough to hang 'em twice over," Spike stated with cold emphasis and relapsed into silence.

"This beef killin'," J.G. observed, in that strangely quiet tone that so little matched the state of mind he had been in lately, "looks like spite work to me.

There's been no trouble with the Hobble-O 't I know of. And daw-gone it, I always put Shep Taylor down as a pretty straight kinda fellow."

"Foxy. If it's them hind quarters you're thinkin' of, I can see through that all right. They work fast and they work at night mostly. Skin out the hind quarters, throw 'em on a pack horse and get to hell outa there. Only takes a few minutes to do that and they're gone. Slip them hind quarters into a freight load uh beef, and who the hell's goin' to know which from t'other? Front quarters ain't worth quite as much, either."

He smoked, again threw out an expressive hand. "It's a cinch," he summed up his reconstruction.

"Wel-l, mebby so. Workin' in the night like that—they must be daw-goned good shots to plug every critter right between the eyes. Don't vary an inch one way or the other, far as I've seen."

Milt shrugged. "Starlight nights, it ain't so hard to do. Locate your cattle just before dark, and when you go after 'em, ride up easy. Most everyone has got white on their faces, you'll notice. Get close and watch your chance. A critter'll turn and look at yuh—if you're up close, it's no trick at all to drop him in his tracks. Nothing to it. Not if a man's any shot at all."

"Looks reasonable," J.G. admitted. "What proof you got as to who done it, Milt?"

"Well, me and Spike's been scoutin' around considerable lately. You might say we caught 'em in the act. Rode down a coulee just about three minutes after they'd left. This was in broad daylight, J.G.—before dark, anyway. We come on the carcass, fresh killed, and took after 'em. Pretty brushy on down farther, but we trailed 'em to where they crossed over a little ridge. It was Shep Taylor, all right. I'd know him far as I could see him. Snuffle was with him. They had a pack horse."

"You jumped 'em, I s'pose?"

Milt shook his head. "Well, no, we didn't. It was a Flying U critter. If it had been one of mine—but it was off up this way, farther north than Lazy Ladder stock is liable to range. No, we moseyed on home. But I'm putting you wise, J.G.—just in case you didn't have a line on who was doing it."

"Much obliged, Milt. No, I ain't had it figured out yet." J.G. looked at his pipe, tapped out the hot ash against the door jamb and put the pipe in his pocket. "The boys has been scoutin' around some themselves," he added. "Found plenty of sign, but it never pointed to any particular person. Might of been most anyone."

"Well, I know damn good and well who's doing it." Milt looked at the older man measuringly. "Maybe you're willing to let 'em get away with it, J.G. Looks like it. Far as I can see, the Flying U hasn't turned a hand to stop it." He got up, pinched out his cigarette and ground the stub under his heel. "You can suit yourself, of course—"

"What you think we ought to do, Milt?" The mildness of his tone would have widened the eyes of any one of his cowboys.

"What am I goin' to do?" Milt looked down at him with a crooked smile. "There's only one thing *to* do, isn't there? Turn 'em in." He hesitated. "Uh course, I hate it like the devil—on account of Shep's family. But them boys—now's the time to learn 'em not to be so damn free with other folks' stock. Let the old man git away with this and there's two fine outlaws comin' up. Them kids'll be swinging a wide loop themselves, three or four years from now. They're learnin' fast, them little buggers."

"Be purty daw-goned tough on the old lady—and the girl."

"Tough on the old lady, yes. But she'd no business marryin' a damn thief. The girl—well, if it wasn't for her *being* a girl—" He looked down at J.G. sitting humped on the doorstep, his hands unconsciously groping again for pipe and tobacco.

"It sure beats me," Milt said impatiently, "how you folks over here never seemed to get wise to what's going on. You live as close to the Hobble-O as I do. How come you ain't got next to 'em before now? That girl's workin' hand in glove with the old man. Acts as lookout—I know that, for a fact. But uh course, being a girl, I reckon there ain't much can be done about it."

"Might string her up alongside her dad," J.G. suggested. "Might make quite an object lesson."

Drawing on his gloves, Milt stiffened. His eyes flashed a glance at Spike Reilly before they rested suspiciously on J.G.'s face. "Might stir up a hell of a stink," he grunted. "I ain't a fool, quite. We've got a way of handling rustlers in this country. It's been used before and it can be again. But that ain't saying—" He broke off with an uneasy laugh. "Hell, this thing has got me so jumpy I can't even see a joke when it's labeled. I don't like kidding about it. I can tell you that."

"When you figuring on havin' your necktie party, Milt?" J.G. rose, as Milt swung easily into the saddle.

"That's up to Dave Burch." Milt's tone was surly. "I might turn in and settle this thing myself, but that ain't my style. I don't go for these badman tactics myself. I'm goin' to report my loss to Dave. I did think," he added, with sarcasm, "you might want to put in with me on it. Make a stronger case. You suit yourself, though."

"Well, I'll think about it," J.G. promised without enthusiasm. "Daw-gone it, Shep's been a purty good neighbor though—"

Milt's laugh was a slur. "Yeh, he sure has been payin' you a fine compliment, J.G. He'd rather have your beef than his own, any old time. If that's the way you like to have it, why that's your funeral." He lifted a gloved hand, turned it in the casual gesture of farewell and trotted his horse down to the corral, Spike Reilly following close behind.

This time Milt pulled up, grinning with acrid humor. "Your old lion has just about turned sheep on yuh, I see," he remarked, by way of opening the subject which filled his mind. "That, or he's made some kinda dicker with the Hobble-O to supply 'em with hind quarters of beef as long as the supply lasts. Damned if I can figure out which it is."

"How's that?" The rising inflection of Weary's voice

sharpened his tone almost to a challenge. "I don't sabe you, Milt."

"Yuh don't? I s'pose you don't know anything that's been going on around here. What you fellows been doing all winter and spring, anyway? Layin' with your heads under the blankets? My God, you oughta lose every hoof on the range! I'll gamble you ain't been outa this coulee since fall round-up. You don't know how the Hobble-O's been butcherin' Flying U beef right and left—that's a cinch. Or maybe you're in cahoots—"

"Easy on that kinda talk, Milt Cummings!" Cal Emmett bristled and started to climb down off the fence.

"Aw, keep your shirt on, Cal." Milt salved the statement, half laughing. "On the square, it made me so damn sore to see old J.G. set there and suck his pipe like he was hearin' good news, all the while I was talkin', I've got to blow off or bust."

"Maybe you better bust," Weary suggested dryly. "We've had about all the blowing off around here we can stand. What yuh know, Milt?"

"I know it looks damn funny to me, the way the Flyin' U lets itself be robbed right and left and never makes a move to stop it," Milt said bluntly, twisting the reins around the saddle horn, that his hands might be free to roll another smoke. "Here I've been ridin' day and night, the last month, getting the goods on the Hobble-O. Not a day passed that I didn't see plenty of Flyin' U carcasses—and yet I never run across a one of you boys on the prowl to see who was doing the butchering. I've got all the proof I want, now—and we rode over today to kinda get together with you folks and make a clean-up." While he rolled the tobacco tightly into its little paper cylinder, he eyed the boys with questioning contempt.

"Looks like your boss is going to set and take it, but I'm damned if I thought you fellows would stand back and let Shep Taylor or anybody else steal cattle right under your noses. I'd have bet anything I got you'd be ready to wipe out that damned thievin' bunch. What I can't understand—"

"J.G.'s the boss around here," Shorty broke in on him. "He don't go off half-cocked, without actual proof. So far, we ain't been able to pin it on—"

"You ain't? You're a hell of a bunch, ain't yuh? Didn't take *me* long to pin it where it belongs. I'm going to turn 'em over to the Vigilantes. You going to back my play or are yuh going to roost on a rail like a bunch of damned chicadees and let other folks do all the dirty work, cleaning up the range for yuh?"

"No use getting snorty, Milt," Weary protested mildly. "J.G.'s collectin' evidence. When he gets a cinch on who's doing it, there's liable to be quite a dust raised. But we don't go agin his orders, not for you or anybody else. Whatever else we may do, this outfit sticks together. You know that."

"Like hell!" Milt looked disgusted. "How about that Bennett rooster? He stuck—in a pig's wrist!"

"Chip? He had to go back to Colorado. His mother left him some property that had to be settled," Weary informed him stiffly.

"Huh! He sure must have settled it damn quick. He's got a job with Butch Lewis, breakin' horses. Saw him there the other day, big as life. I thought it was damn funny he'd quit this bunch and throw in with Big Butch. Must be the way you fellows stick together!" He snorted. "Always knew he was an outlaw."

With that jibe, he slid straight in the saddle and spurred his horse into a gallop from the first jump; the way Milt usually started off. Spike rode after him, a sneering backward glance flung over his shoulder.

Dickybird and Weary hit the ground together, glaring after Milt. "Too damn yella to stay and let me take a crack at him for that!" raged Weary.

"When I see that man again," Dickybird said slowly, teetering on his little feet as he watched Milt out of sight, "he'll take that back or else I'll kill him." And though he said it quietly, Cal Emmett shivered.

XI

THE FIRST REAL CLUE

CHIP PULLED OPEN THE CABIN DOOR AND STOOD looking out, warm sunlight on his lean, tanned face. Behind him sounded the chuckling laugh grown familiar in the last week.

"Well, how about it, kid? Feel like tacklin' a bronc this morning?"

Chip turned his head to look at Butch. In spite of his seventy-three inches plus his high-heeled riding boots, his glance lifted before his brownish hazel eyes met Butch's light blue ones. "No, I don't think so. Thanks all the same, but I've got a job of my own, Butch."

Butch's light eyes hardened perceptibly. "Afraid you'll git a bad name, workin' for me; is that it?"

"Not on your life. If I wanted the job, I'd take it quick enough. But I've got other fish to fry, right now, Butch. You know that."

Butch's fingers were busy with a cigarette. He finished it, got it going before he spoke. "Chasin' beef rustlers, huh? Well, yuh don't have t' go far to find 'em, kid. Not if yuh ride in the right direction."

"That's your theory."

"One theory's good as another, I reckon. What you figure on doin'?"

Chip lifted a foot, drew a match along the boot heel. "Oh—just start out and ride, I guess."

"You won't find nothin' that way, kid. A bullet, maybe."

"That," said Chip, blowing out the match, "is a chance a fellow has to take."

"Goin' to drag that colt along?"

"You bet your life. Little Silver's going right where I go, long as we're both able to travel." A new vibrancy was in Chip's tone.

Butch laughed. "I got the name of being a horse thief, kid, but you could leave that colt here with me and he'd be dead safe till you come after him."

"I know that. I want him along, though. I—I like the darned little skeezicks, Butch. He's lots of company for a fellow."

"Oh, all right. When you get your belly full of chasin' around, come back. Your job'll be open."

Riding out of the basin with his outfit, Chip wondered how Big Butch had got the name of being an outlaw. He certainly had been fine, this past week; no more outlaw than Weary or any of the rest of them. The way he had doctored that arm of Chip's—why, he wasn't half as rough as Polly Taylor had been. Butch had laughed when he took out those stitches. Said Polly must have thought she was mending a mitten when she sewed up that cut.

That remark returned now to Chip, as he rode out of the canyon. The idea of Polly Taylor doing anything so domestic as mending mittens struck him as something grotesque. He tried to picture her in a ruffled dress, sitting beside a sunny window sewing. The shine of gold over her hair where the sun caught it he could see all right, but not Polly mending mittens or anything else. He had a much more vivid picture of her lying up above him in the rocks somewhere, watching Butch's place over the front sight of her rifle.

That was queer too. Butch seemed to think she was up to some devilment. Thought she was helping her dad rustle beef—at least, he had hinted it. Chip tried to see Polly in that role, and he had to admit that certain facts fitted into the picture; everything except his deep-seated conviction that she was honest. Still, what was she doing there so close, when he had the scrap with that fellow under the bank? That couldn't have been her father, because Chip hadn't felt any whiskers. Might have been Snuffle Jones, though. Seemed about the same size and build, as nearly as

Chip could recall those few dazed seconds. If it were Snuffle, that would account for Polly being so close. Only, he couldn't believe Polly Taylor was a thief.

But his thoughts were not long with Polly Taylor. He was riding back into the canyons he knew, following a fresh theory which he had worked out in the long wakeful nights while Big Butch and his men snored in their bunks. Over and over again he retraced his days of fruitless searching for clues, trying to discover what stood out as the most noticeable feature of the killings. He had passed by the glaring fact that all the cattle had borne the Flying U brand; that was, of course, what brought him down here. There must be something else. . . .

One night he had found the elusive thread of coincidence. Never had he noticed any horse tracks around the kills. Now that he thought of it, that was mighty strange, because pack horses must have been used to carry the meat. In some places, there must have been several horses used, because two hind quarters would be a load for any horse. And there hadn't been any tracks. He was sure of that now, though he had been looking for horsemen and had not watched the ground very closely as he rode.

Another thing he had decided was that all the killings had been done within a radius of ten or twelve miles. All the Flying U beef, that is. Milt Cummings, stopping at the cabin a night or two ago, had told of losing a good many cattle, but they ranged off the other side of the Hobble-O Ranch and had nothing to do with the case. It was the Flying U cattle, drifting deepest into the Badlands, that he was thinking of now. He meant to find out, if he could, why the butchers had kept to one part of the breaks, and what were the most feasible trails out of there with loaded horses.

Before, he had been hampered by the belief that Butch Lewis was behind the killings. He had watched the likely places, hoping to catch him in the act. Now he was just as certain that Butch had nothing to do with it. He wasn't going to tie himself up to any fixed idea again. If the Hobble-O were rustling beef, the trail would have to lead to them. He'd made a damned mess of things so far, because he'd thought he knew all about it and had only to collect proof. This was going to be different. He'd look for clues and follow them, even if they led him straight back to the Flying U.

Down in these sheltered canyons the air was warm and springlike, and except on the northern slopes, where the sun did not strike, the snow was nearly gone. He couldn't blame the cattle for hunting these sheltered basins when the winter winds howled across the open land, nor could he wonder why Big Butch had burrowed into his little hidden valley with his stock. Since he never kept one bunch of horses very long, Butch didn't need much range, and the location he had chosen was fine for his purpose. Let the granny gossips talk their tongues off. They couldn't make Chip believe any of their yarns about Butch. When he cleaned up this beef rustling, maybe he'd go back and take Butch up on that offer of a job.

But even while he told himself that, thinking he meant it, in the back of his mind he was wondering what the boys were doing today, and what they thought of the way he had pulled out without a word. He'd bet Weary wasn't fooled a minute. Maybe they were scouting around looking for him that day he saw them. They'd know darned well he wasn't going to pull out and leave the country until this thing was cleared up.

Traveling steadily back the way he had come, by noon he reached a nameless canyon fixed forever in his memory by what had happened here last summer. It was farther down this same canyon where he had held up Cash Farley and his cronies, as they were coming back after a few stolen horses that had broken away from the herd in a thunderstorm and were making for the ranch. It was over north of this canyon where he had fallen almost into the arms of the beef butcher in the fog.

Now, in the light of his clearer understanding, this place seemed especially important. Before, he had passed it by because he was convinced that Butch Lewis was behind the killings, but with Butch out of it, he saw the place from a new angle. Down this canyon there must be a trail of some sort leading out toward the Larb Hills and the country beyond. If the killers had packed meat out this way, he'd find it out, because somewhere along the trail they must have left some evidence of their passing; and if it were there, he told himself grimly, he'd see it. He wasn't riding with his eyes glued to field glasses this time.

Where he had camped last summer, when he was trailing the stolen horses, he stopped again and measured a pint of oats into each nose bag. Just a snack, but it would give the horses heart for the trail ahead. Even little Silver had a handful just to make him feel grown-up, though he forgot his dignity and begged for sugar when Chip took off the nose bag and made ready to start on.

Down the boxlike ravine and into the narrow winding gorge Chip rode, watching for sign. Around the clump of junipers where last summer he had waited until the three outlaws rode into range of his rifle. Beyond that point he never had been, and his nerves tingled now as he rode into the bottle-neck pass that looked as if it were tightly stoppered with granite just around the next turn. But a hundred horses had gone this way last summer and had never been seen again by the Flying U, so there must be a way out.

Horses had gone this way just before the storm, though he could not tell how many, for there were no tracks. Yet his own three horses left plain hoofprints in the hard-packed sand that covered the fissure's floor, except where rock outcropping streaked across. An eerie zigzag crack in the hills it was, where the horses walked uneasily, ears tilted forward expectantly, eyes alert for anything that moved.

Nothing did, save themselves. They emerged from that dark and gloomy gorge into a sunny sage-covered flat where tufts of grass were showing green in the shelter of the bushes. The trail might cross to the hills beyond, or it might not. Chip pulled up to scan this baldly open valley before he went any farther and to roll himself a cigarette. It was while he was holding a match flame to the tobacco that little Silver stepped aside to see what was to be had in the way of browsing, walking along the rough shoulder of the gorge through which they had come.

With fond indulgent eyes, Chip watched the colt go nosing and nipping along, grace in every movement he made. He laughed when Silver sniffed at something on the ground and lifted his nose high in air with lip turned back, the picture of disgust. But when the colt persisted in pawing and snuffing, he stepped off Mike and went to see just what the thing was.

A piece of cowhide, roughly round and deeply cupped, a broken rawhide string dangling from a row of slits near the outer edge. "Huh!" snorted Chip and picked it up from under little Silver's disdainful nose. "Looks like you're worth your oats today, young feller." He turned the object over, and studied it. "I'd tell a man you are!" he cried and gave the colt a boyish hug. "You've sure called the turn this time. Know that?"

Never in his life had he seen such a thing, yet he knew exactly what it was and how it had been used. It was a "boot" designed to pull over a horse's foot and muffle his tracks. Drawn around the ankle above the hoof and tied there, it would last a long while, Chip supposed; when it wore through—well, hides were cheap and easy to get. It would be a simple matter to fashion another.

A simple trick. He should have suspected it long

ago. Perhaps he would have, if he had not been all the while looking for the riders themselves. He wondered if the thieves had worried over this boot when they found the string had broken. They must do their traveling at night, not to have noticed it, and that was probably why he never had any luck finding them. Except that man in the fog, and that struck him as being an impromptu performance with no direct bearing on the others. For one thing, the man had been alone and he had not had a pack horse with him. There had been only the one horse galloping away in the fog, and the hoofbeats certainly had not sounded muffled. Dazed as he had been, he remembered the clink of shoes striking rock.

This was a different matter. Someone had come this way with cowhide boots on his horse. He bent and studied the ground, wondering a little if the wind might not have blown that boot over against the hill. He thought not. Here in the shade a little snow still lay, and under the boot was a tiny bare spot. It had lain up against a small, scraggy sage bush fairly well protected from the wind. He thought it must have dropped there before the storm.

It looked, too, as though the travel had been close alongside the hill, heading south from the gorge. Chip would have struck out east, thinking they had gone that way. But now that he knew what to look for, he could see several faintly dimpled depressions in the sand between the shallow drifts; marks easily overlooked unless one knew their meaning.

With a light of excitement in his eyes, he hurried

back to Mike, mounted and reined in close to the bold rocky bluff and rode warily, heading south.

XII
BEEF HAULIN'S OVER

AT A POINT WHERE THE VALLEY EDGE WAS BROKEN into rocky gullies and steep, water-worn little ridges impossible to climb, Chip pulled up to examine more closely the possibilities of a trail through. At first, it seemed all further progress was blocked. Not one of those gullies was passable for a burro, much less a horse. The gaunt shoulder of the butte came down upon his right—no possible way of getting over that, even if it would not lead him back into the hills. The beef went out east; he was sure of that now, just as he was sure those hooded tracks had come this way.

He looked back, studying the way he had come, two creases deepening between his straight dark eyebrows. The muffled tracks he was trying to follow might be mostly seen with his imagination, but the imprints of his two horses and the colt were certainly plain enough. He couldn't advertise himself any better, even if he chalked his name on the rocks as he rode. Little Silver's tracks were a dead give-away.

That disquieting thought made him wary; that, and the way Mike was acting, turning his head to stare back along the way they had come. He looked again for a way forward, and finally—because there was no other possible outlet—urged Mike into a V-shaped notch in the wall beside him. Solid rock it was, the bottom so narrow the horses had barely room to set their feet. But it was a shelter, and when he had gone a couple of hundred yards along it he slipped off, tied the colt to Jeff's pack, and ran down the crevice to the opening, his rifle swinging from his hand.

Silence and the long shadow of the butte upon the little valley greeted him as he peered cautiously out, and he half turned to go back, calling himself a fool for his fears. No one would be following him. That was just a crazy notion he had got somehow. But he did not go back at once. Instead, he scrambled up the north side of the notch, to where he had glimpsed a little clump of half-starved sage, and crouched there on a precariously narrow knob, where a bit of earth had found lodgment and the bushes fought for meager life.

Fifteen or twenty feet above his horses' tracks, he had a clear sweep of the valley, though his view of the trail was cut off by a bulge in the bluff wall a few hundred yards away. As he settled himself to watch, a jackrabbit bounced into sight and ran for a few rods before he kicked himself out of range among the rocks of the nearest gully.

Barely had he settled himself when a rider appeared around the bulging rock, coming ahead cautiously with his rifle at half aim, looking and craning. But he wasn't looking for that jackrabbit, Chip would bet money on that. He rode as if he knew all about the barrier ahead and the broken country no horse could cross to reach the valley. He seemed all prepared to meet someone. And as he drew nearer, another detail impressed itself upon the mind of the watcher. The horse wore boots of cowhide, hairy side out, and the rider reined him close against the hill, well to one side of the tracks clean-cut there in the sand.

Chip's thumb drew back the hammer of his gun. His mouth pinched in at the corners, then his head lifted. "Hey! Where d'you think you're going?" he called down peremptorily, spoiling the perfect ambush.

For answer, the fellow swung up his rifle and fired. The bullet kicked rock dust against Chip's face before it whined off into the gully. He fired again, three quick shots before Chip squeezed the trigger and dropped him out of the saddle.

Short and sharp as it was, Chip saw how his hand was shaking when he lifted it to feel the spot on his cheekbone where a bit of granite had struck and knocked off the skin. No use—he never would get used to this gun-fighting. Yet a man had to fight, if he would live in this country. It was like war, he told himself, as he slid down from his perch. The law didn't reach out into the wild places. A man had to fight his battles as best he could. No use being squeamish about it—the man was a thief or he wouldn't have those things on his horse's feet. And he was a killer, too. His actions proved that.

Yet Chip went reluctantly out to see what could be done for the fellow. He was so slow about it that by the time he got out of the crevice where he could see, there was neither horse nor man to be seen anywhere.

Puzzled; suspicious of some trick to call him out into the open, he hugged the rock and made his way cautiously along to the swelling shoulder of the bluff. Beside the spot where the man had fallen he paused to inspect the ground with quick darting glances, afraid to take his eyes for more than a second from the trail. The scuffed imprint was there, all right, and a reddish stain on the ground. The fall was no fake then. At the bulge he paused again, listening, then inched his way around where he could see. And there went the fellow, loping back along the way he had come, riding like a drunken man but making good speed.

Chip scowled and watched him go. He had been alone, then. Just a spy upon his movements, trailing him up and anxious to get a shot at him. It wasn't a pleasant thought, but presently Chip shrugged and went back to his horses. After all, his business was to find out who had been packing beef out on horses wearing cowhide boots. Let the damned spy go. He guessed the fellow had enough to hold him for a while. The way he was sifting out of sight, he wasn't liable to be back.

With his mind more at ease—because now he knew that he was on the right track—he went on, following the crevice, although it seemed to be doubling back into the hills again. Later he saw why. In the days when the land was in the making, this high barren butte had been split and twisted in some titanic upheaval after it had probably considered itself full grown and settled for life. The crack he followed ended suddenly in a wider ravine, which ran eastward and a little south, as Chip judged by the sun and the fine old watch that had been his father's. And the ravine opened out into a deep little coulee which lay back in the butte, yawning widely at the same valley he had left, but farther around its southern end.

Now he saw the reason for the apparently aimless detour. Within four or five miles he had come into new country completely removed from the scene of the butcherings. The high rocky butte formed a natural barrier with no discernible connection between this coulee and the canyon he had left back there. But that there was a connection he had just proved to himself; and by all the laws of logic, he should find some tangible clue to the rustlers right here in this coulee. A camp, probably. They'd need someplace to store their beef until they could gather a load to haul out. There ought to be a wagon road out of here and a cabin, at least.

The road, when he found it, was a deeply rutted track winding down through the willow fringe that bordered a small creek. "Not much travel, but what there is has been heavy, all right," he decided, and followed the road back up the coulee until he saw the corner of a cabin roof against sheer cliff. It reminded him of the way Big Butch's cabin was located; reminded him too of a man with his back to the wall, forcing his enemies to come at him in front. It had a wary, watchful look—and yet when he tied his horse in a thicket and slipped through the willows to where he had a fair, close view of the place, it looked innocent enough with its corrals and haystack. Like somebody's line camp, he thought dubiously; or like some nester who had settled in there and gotten a fair foothold.

Smoke was rising from the stovepipe, so he slipped like an Indian through the bushes and reached the stable without once showing himself, got inside through a back window and looked the place over. Two sets of harness with four-horse lines was his only reward there. He climbed out again and went to investigate the big, high-boxed wagon that stood under a shed at the stable's south end. One look was all he needed there. A stained and greasy canvas, commonly called a tarp in the range country, lay loosely folded inside; and there was grease on the inside of the end gate where beef had been slid in over it.

"And this lets the Hobble-O out of it, slick as a whistle," Chip told himself, and felt a glow of satisfaction in the thought. All he needed now was to find where they cached the beef while they made up a load—two or three nights' stealing, he estimated it roughly—and to learn who owned this camp. The horses were out in pasture, so he'd have to go down there to read their brand—and if the thieves were smart, they wouldn't show their own brands on their stock, anyway.

He hunted as thoroughly as he dared for a cellar, or even a cave, but without any success. So presently he made his way stealthily back to his horses, mounted Mike and rode up the trail to the corral, left them there and walked on to the cabin, a fresh-made cigarette between his lips.

"And what the hell do *you* want?" a bony, bow-legged old fellow demanded from the suddenly opened door. He had a double-barreled shotgun in his hands and his yellowish eyes set close to a high beak of a nose gave him the look of a hawk on the watch for a chicken.

Chip's engaging grin gave no hint of his purpose, but it was brief and left his face grimly anxious. "If you're always on the job like this, old-timer, I guess the boys didn't lie about you, after all. Got any more private place for my horses than that damned open-face corral?"

The old man hesitated, lowered the gun a trifle. "On the dodge, be yuh?" He looked Chip over suspiciously. "Who'n hell sent yuh here? I don't want no trouble."

"You sure don't hate it any worse than I do," Chip declared, walking unconcernedly up to the door. "I don't mind layin' out in the hills—but hell, a fellow's got to sleep sometime, and cook himself a hot meal. I certainly do admire that smoke coming out of your stovepipe, Mister." He pushed back his big gray hat, sighing as he drew his fingers across his forehead.

"Where you from?"

"Well, the last roof I slept under belonged to Big Butch," he said cautiously.

"He's a friend of yours?"

"Well, he wished me luck when I rode off. That's as friendly as it's safe to be in this country, I guess."

The old man grunted and stepped aside, motioning for Chip to enter. "Which way'd you come over?" he wanted to know, standing his gun behind the door. "Past Milt's, or through the saddle-string?"

"Saddle-string," Chip told him promptly, thinking

that a good name for the cleft he had followed through the butte. "When I think it's safe to tackle the river again, I may go by Milt's place. I only stopped for a cup of hot coffee, if you've got it handy. I was just kidding about wanting to sleep here. I'd rather den up in the hills—and besides, I wouldn't want to be here alone when you have to take another load out."

The old man cocked an eyebrow at that, but he made no comment. "Coffee's bilin'," he said gruffly. "There's a kittle uh beans. Help yourself. I jest et."

"Thanks. A fellow on the go all the while never gets to cook a mess of beans." With the practiced ease of a man used to baching, he went over to the wash bench, dipped water from the wooden bucket standing there and washed his face and hands, combing his hair by the sense of feeling, because there was no glass in sight anywhere. He'd have to be careful, he thought, while he put his little black comb in its case and slipped it into his pocket. That old hellion would certainly feed him a load of buckshot if he made a slip.

In guarded silence he turned to the cupboard and got himself a plate, filled it at the stove and poured himself a cup of coffee. While he spooned in brown sugar, he lifted his glance and studied his host with a level, untroubled look that was almost a challenge. Not so old after all, he decided. Not as old as J.G. by five years, if he were any judge. It was the man's boniness and his dirty unkemptness that gave him the appearance of age. Chip felt better about it, somehow.

"What's Butch doin' now?" the man asked abruptly, watching Chip like the hawk he resembled.

"Going to start in gentling a bunch of broomtails. He just sent quite a bunch south, a couple of weeks ago." Only two weeks? It seemed like six months since he had left the Flying U. But he brought his thoughts back to the present moment. He'd have to keep his wits about him. Couldn't let them go wool-gathering now. The old devil was watching him. Going to try and catch him up on something.

But that was not apparent. The man was nodding his head and stroking his dingy whiskers thoughtfully. "Who's he got workin' for 'im now?" The question was not so casual as he wanted it to appear. His eyes spoiled that.

Chip finished his drink and set down the cup. "Sime and Sam and Flicker, in camp now. The rest are on the drive."

"Ahuh." He combed his whiskers meditatively. "Seen Milt lately?"

"Three or four days ago. Friday, I believe it was." Chip looked up from his plate. "Milt claims the Hobble-O has been getting away with his cattle."

"He-he-he!" cackled Hawk-eyes. And then, "When's he aimin to pull that there necktie party over 't the Hobble-O? By cracky I wanta be there when that comes off?" His grimy face suddenly became a mask of malevolence. "I ain't fergot the time old Shep run me off'n the ranch with a rifle. Be better'n a meal uh vittles to watch him dance on air." He swore horribly, with a fluent blasphemy that made Chip's flesh crawl.

But nerves must be steady now. Like a landslide after the long calm, enlightenment rushed in upon him. As if the whole vile scheme had been carefully explained to him, he saw it all. The Hobble-O Ranch and range, which would double the Lazy Ladder holdings. But Milt Cummings! Even his dislike of Mitt had never held a suspicion of his honesty. Why, Weary had worked for Milt and liked him just fine. The fiendish cunning of the plot stunned him, turned him physically sick. He pushed back his plate, unable to swallow another mouthful.

Lucky for him that Hawk-eyes was absorbed in his own poisonous gloating: "—tell 'im, 'Kick an' be damned. Shep,' I'll say, 'yuh won't never kick Skelp Turner agin—' "

Chip's back hair prickled at the roots. Skelp Turner! He'd heard the boys talk about Skelp, who had lived with the Indians and was reputed to have white men's scalps stretched on little hooks and hoarded as trophies of the hunt. Five scalps, Slim had declared, and one of them had long yellow hair. . . .

He forced the loathing out of his eyes, forced his voice to speak calmly. "But Milt'll be sending you out with another load of beef pretty quick now, won't he, Skelp?"

Skelp ripped out an obscene oath. "If he does, and goes t' work and strings Shep Taylor up while I'm gone, I'll skin 'im alive!" Then he chuckled, at ease again. "Shucks, what'm I fussin' about? Beef haulin's over, if this good weather keeps up. That's why he's aimin' to clean out the Hobble-O. Couldn't haul no beef after that." He pried off a chew of tobacco, looking like a wolf yanking at a tough tendon. "How's the Flyin' U settin'? Milt say what fer luck he's had, ringin' them in on the hangin'?"

Chip set his teeth and busied himself with a cigarette. "No, he didn't say," he answered that, when he could trust his voice. "I don't believe he'd been over there yet." And to cover his ignorance of Milt's movements, "They sure have lost a lot of cattle, all right. Milt played foxy there. Just the hind quarters skinned out—I'll bet that outfit's right on the warpath."

"He-he-he!" tittered Skelp, and Chip could scarcely keep his hands off the wretch's throat. "Foxy as they make 'em. Laid his plans quick as he heard about the Hobble-O gittin' that beef contract. *He-he-he!* Now 't round-up's comin' on purty soon, he'll let the neighbors come in an' clean up for 'im." In great detail he dwelt upon the proposed cleaning up, until Chip rose tight-lipped, unable to bear more.

"What'n hell ails yuh?" Skelp broke off to demand fretfully. "What yuh lookin' so squawmish about? Ain't yuh never saw a hangin'?"

"Your damn beans are sour," Chip grunted, picking up his hat and heading for the door. "Come on, Skelp. We better be moving. Milt'll beat you to it if you don't look out."

Skelp swore and picked up his shotgun. "Thought you was on the dodge." He peered sharply into Chip's face.

"I'm not dodging Milt Cummings," Chip retorted. "I want to know what his plans are. If he's through peddling beef, he'll move quick." He looked at Skelp with a sardonic gleam in his eyes. "Better hurry—you're liable to miss the show!"

"Like hell! Milt promised me—"

But he darted out ahead of Chip, and he almost trotted on his way to the corral.

XIII

SEVENTY BELOW ZERO

WHILE SKELP TOOK LONG STEPS TO HIS SADDLE horse, staked on a grassy flat just beyond the willows back of the corral, Chip made certain preparations of his own and waited, fighting down an uneasy feeling that this was too easy not to have a slip-up later on. It seemed almost incredible that Skelp Turner's obsession for revenge would rob him of all caution toward a stranger. He had every reason to be wary. He was, at first. It was talking about Shep Taylor that had thrown him off guard, made him accept Chip as one of the gang without any proof whatever; yet he must have lived by suspicion and wolfish cunning to have survived so long. Unless he was a little cracked on the subject of Shep Taylor—Chip drew a deep, worried breath, hoping that was the solution.

Skelp came bow-legging back with a depressed little sorrel, muttering to himself an imaginary dialogue which was to take place between himself and Shep Taylor, just before the noose tightened around Shep's neck; rehearsing iniquitous taunts which he mouthed like savory morsels, tittering to himself while he saddled. He mounted and reined into a faint stock trail, wandering aimlessly toward the mouth of a canyon vaguely outlined against the hills, as the sun swung farther toward the west.

He was still mumbling into his ragged whiskers when Chip, riding behind him, lifted his coiled rope from where he had hung it over the saddle horn, settled himself with feet firm in the stirrups and softly shook out his loop.

Swift as a striking rattler he swung the loop once and shot it straight forward. So quick was the throw that when Skelp heard the swish of the rope the loop was already tightening around his gaunt body, pinning both arms to his sides, and he was being yanked off his horse backward as Mike swung off and braced himself for the shock. One yelp of astonishment died in Skelp's throat when he hit the ground.

The thud of his fall drowned the fainter thud of Chip's boots on gravel, as he jumped off and ran forward, piggin string between his clenched teeth. Like a man after the championship prize in a roping contest, he threw himself on Skelp, grabbed his arms and pulled them together behind him and took his half hitches with the practiced twist and yank of a veteran. The little sorrel had run a few steps and turned, eyeing the proceedings with flared nostrils and a curious look in his patient eyes.

Chip pulled Skelp's gun out of its holster, caught a glimpse of something at his boot top and pulled out a wicked-looking bowie knife. He felt for a second gun and found it under his left armpit. "You sure don't figure on giving the other fellow a chance," he snorted and searched more carefully. A second knife he sent spinning into the brush. “A rattlesnake’s a gentleman alongside you, you old reprobate,” he observed contemptuously as he stood up.

Abruptly he leaned and slapped a particularly vile epithet back into Skelp’s yellowed teeth. “I’ve listened to all that kind of talk I’m going to,” he grated and gagged Skelp with his own dirty neckerchief. “I oughta kill you as I would a snake, but I won’t. I’ll leave that for Shep Taylor. Get up, damn yuh!”

Tied though he was, Skelp fought savagely with his feet, kicking with amazing force and dexterity, throwing himself about until he seemed to have the legs of a centipede; until Chip rapped him alongside the head with the barrel of his gun and sent him limp as a shot coyote. Whereupon he loaded him onto the little sorrel, tied his feet into the stirrups, roped him to the saddle so he couldn’t fall off, led the sorrel back and tied him to Jeff’s pack and stood surveying his handiwork while he rolled himself a smoke.

His breath came panting, but it was more anger than exhaustion that set him trembling. He could scarcely get the tobacco into its tiny paper trough, after spoiling three papers by tearing off too wide a strip. He felt as though he had just captured alive some loathsome monster whose breath poisoned the air around him, and he could scarcely credit the luck he seemed to have had. The malignant glare which Skelp focused upon him gave him the uneasy sense that this was all too easy and that he would presently find that he had walked straight into a trap set for him.

But that was nerves, and he couldn’t afford to get

jumpy now, when his job was only half done. He forced himself to smoke that cigarette as calmly as if he hadn't a worry in the world, and he even walked over and offered a lump of sugar to little Silver and petted and talked to him a minute. It steadied him to feel the colt's satiny muzzle in his palm, his lip seeking daintily for the last sweet grain; furthermore, it pleased him to show Skelp that catching him wasn't anything to get excited about. Still, he couldn't afford to waste too much time, either. It was well past the middle of the afternoon already and there was no telling what lay before him.

He was thrusting his toe into the stirrup when hoof beats sounded quite close behind him, coming at a trot down the trail from the corral. He had just time to snatch his rifle from its scabbard on the saddle and duck behind a boulder beside the trail when a rider's hat crown appeared above the bushes. Only one, however. Chip swung up his rifle and stepped out into sight again just as Polly Taylor rode up.

She seemed to grasp the situation at a glance. "Well, forever more!" she exclaimed. "*Now* what have you been doing?"

"Well, what does it look like?" Chagrin roughened Chip's voice.

"Looks to me as if you were liable to need some help if you keep on traveling in this direction," Polly retorted briskly. "Why don't you turn and head the other way—back to the Flyin' U?" She looked at Skelp. "That outfit will know how to handle *him*."

Here she was, trying to interfere again in his business. Chip put up his rifle and mounted. "You'd better go on home," he told her, and instantly thought of the man he had turned back with a bullet in him somewhere. "Did you meet anyone? I suppose you trailed me over here." His tone was resentful.

"I didn't meet anyone and I certainly did trail you. You left a spoor like a herd of elephants, so I can't feel swell-headed over it. How'd you manage to get the best of Skelp? He's about the slimiest creature the good Lord ever made—if He did make him. I suppose he's one of the beef rustlers. What are you going to do now, Chip?"

For answer Chip merely lifted his shoulders in the gesture calculated to set presumptuous persons in their places.

It got nothing but a ladylike sniff from Polly. "Still seventy below zero, I see," she observed calmly. "All right, if that's the way you feel. But just remember I'm more deeply concerned in this business than you are. My father's life is worth a lot more than your precious pride. So freeze up and bust, for all I care. I'm going along."

She went. There was no stopping her. She rode behind little Silver, bringing up the rear and keeping a watchful eye on Skelp Turner, her rifle laid across the saddle in front of her. And Chip, conscious of her watchful presence behind him, told himself that he wished to the Lord she'd stay home and mind her own business, and all the while knew in his heart that he was glad she was there. There wouldn't be anyone slipping up behind him, maybe shooting him in the back, while she was on guard.

When the roofs of the Lazy Ladder buildings showed black against the setting sun, a hay corral with two old stacks just ahead, his manner was almost gentle when he swung Mike around and rode back to her.

"I'm going to leave you here behind these haystacks with Skelp," he said. "Keep out of sight—but if you hear shooting, make tracks out of here."

"I understand," she answered meekly.

"Whatever happens, don't you go mixing into any trouble. You sabe?"

"Of course." But she didn't look at him when she said it.

"Skelp's tied for keeps. He can't do a thing. You'll be all right here." He was uneasy, hating to leave her. He didn't know what she might take it into her head to do. "Don't you take any crazy idea of helping—"

"Why, do you think you may need help?" Her eyes turned questionably upon him.

"No. If I do, it wouldn't do any good. You watch Skelp and the horses for me." He hesitated, gave her a shy, resentful look. "You'll help me a lot right here."

"You—be careful, won't—"

He had touched Mike with the spurs and was gone, loping up the rutted meadow road, a last yellow sun ray pouring down upon him as the sun slipped behind a jagged pinnacle just beyond the ranch. Then he rode into shadow and disappeared around a turn.

It would be madness to attempt to reach the place by stealth; Chip knew better than to try it. He rode up at a leisurely fox trot and stopped at the corral gate. Three saddle horses stood inside, but there were no saddles anywhere around. No one hailed him, no door opened anywhere.

He rode on to the house, where lazy smoke drifted up from the chimney. Still no one appeared, so he dismounted and knocked on the door. Quick steps inside, a pause, and then, "Who is it?" a young voice demanded.

Chip winced a little. A few months ago he had thought that voice the sweetest he had ever heard. Julie Lang—Mrs. Milt Cummings now. His shoulders squared as his chin went up.

"Chip Bennett, Mrs. Cummings. Is your husband at home?"

Before he had finished speaking, the door was wide open and Julie stood there, blue eyes wide as she looked at him. "Oh! I—I never *dreamed* it was you! C-come in, stranger." She smiled when she called him that, but Chip did not smile back.

"I can't stop," he told her brusquely. "I wanted to see Milt."

"Milt—oh, don't you know what horrible—haven't you heard?"

He stared at her. "You mean the Hobble-O?" It was a shot in the dark, but it hit the mark.

Julie shivered. "Milt and the boys went to round up the Cow Island bunch. They left just a little bit ago. Oh, I think it's *horrible* that such things have to happen. But, of course, you can't let folks just go on stealing right and left—" Her starry blue eyes lifted to

Chip's face. He looked down into them but they could not set his pulse leaping now. They could do nothing whatever to him except show him that they were just shiny blue eyes such as a Christmas doll in a store window might own.

His thoughts raced after Milt and his crew, turned to the Hobble-O, to the trail Milt would follow. He was counting hours and minutes, trying to guess how long they would stop in Barr Lang's saloon, drinking whiskey to stiffen their courage. Two seconds, maybe, of silence—but Chip's thoughts had covered the whole gruesome subject during the brief pause.

"How long since they left?"

"Oh, I don't know—fifteen minutes, maybe. If you don't catch them, you'll find them at Uncle Barr's place, I guess. Milt said you boys were all set on it, when I tried to make him give it up and just run them out of the country or something. But he said the Flying U wouldn't stand for that, because you've lost more cattle than he has, even. Have you really, Chip?"

"We lost a plenty. Well, thanks, Jul—Mrs. Cummings. I'll have to be going."

"I think it's awful! But Milt simply *can't* let it go on any longer—"

Chip left her talking there in the doorway. The swift beat of Mike's hoofs must have warned Polly, for she was halfway from the stacks to meet him, her rifle in her hands ready for battle. She looked past Chip, saw he was not followed, and her face went so white all her freckles stood out with startling distinctness.

"What is it? Have they gone to get Dad?"

Chip gave her a quick glance. It was no time for lying. "Gone to round up the Cow Island Vigilantes. You better stay here with Julie. I'll beat them to the ranch—we'll stand 'em off, all right. We'll be ready for them, Polly. Don't you worry. You stay here."

"Like hell," swore Polly, and wheeled Pathfinder in the trail and raced off up the road. Before Chip could stop her, she was lifting a dust banner along the road home. Even while he stared she ripped around a point of rocks and was gone like a scared antelope.

"Little fool!" Chip ground out between his teeth. But a warm light sprang into his eyes and his blood flowed a little faster.

XIV
PRISONER'S LOOSE

SHEP TAYLOR WALKED TO THE FIREPLACE, SPAT INTO the flames and kicked a juniper root in against its mate. He turned and looked at Chip.

"We could stand off a regiment uh soldiers in here," he said, recurring to an argument just ended. "When I built this house outa rock, I calc'lated she'd be solid, and she is. Burned my own lime for the chinkin', had good clean sand right down there by the crick for mortar, and a querry uh rock right alongside uh me. Me and Snuffle done a good job. Built her up high enough for a chamber to hold the raft uh kids we're raisin'. They'll have to burn the roof off the damn place—and even then I don't see how they're goin' to git at us."

He canted a look at his wife, turned and spat again into the fire. "Maw, you hush your bawlin'. You know damn well you'll be givin' that young one the colic, if you go workin' yourself up." And he added for comfort, "I ain't in a mite of danger."

"Oh, I ain't worryin' about you," Maw retorted with a sniff. "I'm worried to death about Polly. Mr. Bennett says she started for home ahead of him and she ain't showed up yet. If any of them hellhounds have got hold of her, there's no tellin' what they'll do."

"I don't see how they could get her," Chip told her, though he had said it before. "I followed right along as fast as I could with my outfit and there was no sign of anyone on the trail. I believe she must have turned off somewhere to do a little scouting on the way." He got up restlessly, picking up hat and short sour-dough coat from a chair.

"I'm going to scout around some myself," he answered Shep's inquiring look. "I hate to stay penned up inside, I don't care how safe it is. If they show up, they'll be shooting. That will give you notice they're here." He looked at Mrs. Taylor. "I don't think this is going to amount to anything at all; when they find out we're expecting them, they'll back off."

"If you see Polly, you send her right in here to me," she told him. "Harve and Ernie, you come right back in here and set down!" She strode toward the doorway into the kitchen, a year-old baby riding astride her bony hip. "Pa, make them young ones stay inside!"

Shep lifted his cud of tobacco and spat juice hastily. "Ernest, you go and set down over there," he sternly commanded the younger, a freckled boy of eight or nine. "Here, Harve, you take this shotgun of old Skelp Turner's, if you want to go out and fight. You can't hit nothin' in the dark with that rifle."

"Aw, I c'n shoot the bill off'n a musketeer with this gun, Pa! It ain't very dark, anyway."

"You do as I tell yuh! Here's the shells Chip took off'n Skelp. You hide in them rocks out there by the woodpile and fill their hides with buckshot if they come to the house. You'll have to fight your way, if you live in this country, and you might just as well start in now as any time."

"Put on your overshoes, Harvey, and wear your mittens till you see 'em comin'," his mother admonished him. "You'll likely have quite a while to wait. They'll hang around Barr Lang's drinkin' and screwin' up their courage till all hours of the night, most likely. Button up your coat good and tie that scarf around your neck."

"I don't want to fight lynchers with no shotgun," Harvey grumbled. "Gosh, you'd think they was chickadees!"

Chip grinned in spite of himself. "Skelp Turner didn't carry a shotgun for chicadees, kid. You see the length of that barrel? And heft one of those shells. That's a young cannon you've got there."

"Anyway," Harve's mother settled the matter unexpectedly, "I may want to use your rifle myself, if the baby ain't too fretful. You be a good boy, Harvey, and do as your father tells you."

A strange family, Chip thought, as they slipped out

of the back door. With such a mother Polly was explained. Pioneer stock: he did not need to be told that. Probably Shep and his wife had stood at loopholes and defended their cabin from Indians not so many years ago. The big-eyed solemnity of the three little tots sitting in a row on a bench beside the fireplace remained long in his memory.

That lean dark woman hushing her baby and crying slow tears over Polly's unaccountable absence one moment, and calmly planning to use a rifle on the unexpected lynching party the next, stirred him with an odd sympathy. Unaccountably he wondered if Abraham Lincoln's mother was like that. And old Shep warming his back and spitting into the fire—but with his rifle lying handy on the mantel and a full belt of ammunition buckled around his middle, the scarred butt of a forty-five drooping over its holster—would be a hard proposition to tackle.

Snuffle Jones, big and swarthy and with an habitual sniff, waited in the kitchen, where he would have a clear view of the stable and corrals. Lacking the element of surprise, Milt Cummings and his bunch would have their work cut out for them, Chip thought. Only Polly was lacking to complete the picture of competent defense.

He wished he knew where Polly was. Saying she must be off scouting around was merely an attempt to ease her mother's worry. Polly knew where Milt and his men had gone and she knew why. She wasn't crazy enough to think she could go to Cow Island and persuade them to give up their plan, and there was no other possible reason for going there. And there was nothing to be found out by riding. Something must have happened to her or she would have been home long before now, for he had traveled more slowly with Jeff and the colt—he would not have hung back for the comfort of Skelp Turner!—and he had been here about an hour; more, he guessed by the stars. Darn the girl! If she had gone to Cow Island, the whole bunch would know the Hobble-O expected them. No telling what they'd do then.

From the rocks by the woodpile Harvey's voice came to him. "Gee whiz, how long have we got to wait?"

"No telling, Harve." Chip had made a tour of the yard and corrals just to familiarize himself with the place, and had swung back near the house. "They might be along any minute now or maybe not for two hours."

"Will they come a-whoopin' and a-yellin', or will they kinda sneak up on us?"

"That depends on how much they've been drinking, I guess."

"Gee, I wish they'd hurry up and come," the boy complained. "It's darned cold, layin' here on the watch."

"You could go in and get warm," Chip suggested. "I'm going to prowl down the road a ways. You'll hear a shot if they show up."

Without waiting to see what the boy did, he walked on, down past the rock storehouse where Taylor had put Skelp to wait until they decided what to do with him. Chip halted there, half tempted to go in and take a look at the prisoner. But he would have to strike a match to see anything, and he thought it would be just as well not to show a light outside the house just then. Anyway, it wasn't necessary to look. Skelp was tied and the gag was in his mouth, so he couldn't call for help. Yes, and the door was padlocked, Chip remembered now, and old Shep had the key in his pocket; if he wasn't so edgy, he'd have remembered that. The old devil was safe enough.

He went on slowly, not wanting to get too far from the house, yet too restless to remain in one spot. In the clear starlight the coulee wall showed vaguely, without shadows. They'd come by the road, he told himself again. The creek had cutbanks and its windings crowded the road against the west wall of the coulee. They wouldn't want to tackle crossing the creek at night, even if it were possible. They wouldn't see any reason for it, if Polly had stayed away from Cow Island and kept her mouth shut. They'd just ride up quietly, maybe two or three—Milt Cummings probably—with some yarn that would bring Snuffle and old Shep outside, where they could grab them, while the main crowd waited down here somewhere. . . .

It happened so suddenly he did not know what hit him. He was passing a boulder lying close to the road, where it dipped down into a little hollow, and something landed on his head and shoulders, hurling him to the ground. Hands clawed for his throat and a voice snarled like some wild animal fighting and clawing. As he dropped his rifle and threw up his hands to defend himself, one hand brushed against whiskers and clamped down upon a handful.

So he knew it was Skelp. He could tell by the snarling whine in the voice, by the whiskers and by the terrible strength in those fingers.

Chip swung and twisted, brought up his other hand and found Skelp's throat. They rolled together on the frozen ground and the stars Chip saw were red as blood. The beating of a thousand drums was in his ears. Skelp's legs clamped around his so tight that he could not move. The world was bursting like a rocket, but he would not let go. His tortured brain told him to press harder—hard as Skelp was pressing. Skelp had to breathe too. Skelp couldn't live without air in his lungs—Skelp was seeing stars—if he could only dig his thumbs a little deeper—cut off his wind. . . .

He couldn't. He had reached his limit. It wasn't worth while—let Skelp go . . .

The air rushing into his starved lungs strangled Chip. He gasped, groaned, lifted his heavy arms and tried to push off the dead weight that held him down. He blinked and saw the stars far off in their firmament, and they were no longer red as blood but yellow and crisply twinkling. So he had choked Skelp down. He had beaten him to it. And with that thought, he rolled out from under and sat up.

"D' yuh s'pose I killed 'im?" Harvey asked in a sibilant whisper. "Gosh, Chip, he was chokin' the daylights outa yuh! I couldn't make out which was which, for a minute. An then, when I did, I sure slammed 'im. Bent this old shotgun barrel double, I bet!"

Chip got to his feet, stood there swaying groggily. "Good for you, kid. You sure got here in time." He stooped to examine the limp figure at his feet.

"Got here? Hell, I *was* here!" Harvey snorted. "I was right behind yuh. I seen him jump on yuh."

"Get—get a rope." Chip was rubbing his neck where Skelp's fingers had bruised it. "I've got to tie him."

The boy hesitated. "Say, if he ain't dead yet, why don't you shoot him? Pa told Snuffle that's what you'd oughta done in the first place, 'stead of bringin' him here, like you done. He's bad medicine. Go on, Chip."

Chip picked up his rifle and stood leaning on it, while he stared at Harvey. "You don't know what you're talking about. I don't kill men that can't fight back. You march and get that rope."

"I bet you'll wish you killed him before you're through," Harvey prophesied grimly, as he started off. "Pa was sorry he didn't last fall, stid of just runnin' him off'n the ranch. Skelp was after Polly, tryin' to make her marry him—and he's lousy and keeps white men's skelps hangin' up on the wall."

"Don't stand there gabbing. Hurry up."

Left alone, Chip gave Skelp an investigative poke with his boot. The man was limp, inert—dead so far as movement went. Perhaps two knocks on the head within a few hours of one another had been more than even Skelp could stand. Still, a man who could crawl out of those ropes and escape from a stone building locked as that storehouse was would take more killing than that. His heart was beating fairly strong, a minute ago; he'd come out of it all right.

But there was no sign of life, no gasp of returning consciousness. Chip leaned against the bank, the boulder at his back, and proceeded to roll himself a smoke. Soon as Skelp came to, he'd march him up to the house and let the folks watch him. Pity you couldn't kill a skunk like him and think no more about it. It certainly would save a lot of trouble.

Down the coulee there was no sound save the whisper of a keen little breeze that rose in faint gusts and died again. He hadn't really expected the Vigilantes to come for some time yet. About midnight was the time they usually got in their work, according to all he'd heard of them. You couldn't tell, though. It wouldn't do to bank on that.

He smoked half his cigarette before he knelt again to inspect his captive. Still dead to the world. That kid sure must hit hard. What was keeping the little devil, anyway? He could have gathered all the rope on the ranch in the time he had been gone. Chip walked a few steps up the road, peering through the starlight. A fine fix he'd be in, if that lynching party showed up before he had Skelp tied up again!

That thought turned him back to listen for hoofbeats down the coulee. He thought he heard a slight scuffling of gravel near the boulder, but it might have been the breeze; though he hurried a little, in case Skelp was beginning to show signs of life. He did not hurry fast enough. When he had taken the dozen steps to the place where he had left Skelp, the road was empty.

For a few seconds Chip stood motionless, straining

his ears to hear some sound. It was as silent there as though no other human being had been within a mile of the spot. Instinctively he moved back away from the boulder, searching each hiding place with his eyes as he slowly retreated, walking backwards up the road with his six-shooter out, ready to fire at any moving thing he saw.

Luckily he had taken his rifle with him when he took those few steps away from the boulder, looking for Harvey. Had he left it leaning against the rock where he placed it while he made a cigarette, Skelp would have been armed. As it was, he was by no means helpless, as Chip's bruised and aching throat attested. He had the strength of two men and the swiftness of a weasel; a dangerous beast in the dark, likely to spring out from hiding without warning.

Harvey came tardily, trailing a loose coil of rope. "I sure had to hunt," he explained. "There wasn't nothin' but lass rope and what's on the halters, and I'd git a lickin' if I gloomed them. There wasn't nothin' but Maw's clothesline, and I had a dickens of a time untying it. I didn't dast to cut it—Maw'd be mad."

Chip sent him back to his station by the woodpile. For himself, he decided that the rock storehouse would be as good a place as any. He would have a wall at his back, and he could slip around it and cover the corrals and stable as well as the road and house yard. With Skelp loose, he had a double reason for sticking close to the trouble center. No telling what Skelp would take a notion to do now. Something devilish, Chip was willing to bet on that.

XV
THE FLYING U TO THE RESCUE

By the slow march of the stars overhead it was nearly midnight. Two hours or so ago Chip had heard the faint slam of the kitchen door and guessed that Harvey had tired of guard duty and gone in. Soon after that the lights in kitchen and living room went out. Lamplight shone briefly from the upstairs window and was extinguished. Apparently the Taylor family was tucked in for the night. Only Chip knew better than that.

And still no Polly. From his post beside the storehouse, Chip watched the road, looking for the girl. In spite of himself, he forgot the Vigilantes for long minutes at a time and strained his eyes through the darkness, hoping to see that slim little rider on the chunky brown horse come up the trail. Between the slow gusts of wind pushing down over the coulee rim he listened for the quiet hoofbeats of one horse.

So absorbed was he in his worried watching that a sliding shadow disappearing into the blacker shade of the stable failed just at first to register in his mind. It looked like a dog, he thought indifferently—and then he remembered that the Taylors had no dogs.

With long noiseless strides he headed for the spot, which brought him to the far end of the long low stable. There a door opening out of a small corral stood open; a door which he remembered was closed when he left his horses inside. In the corral Skelp

Turner's horse moved uneasily, head up and facing the doorway. Starlight was reflected from his eyes which glowed in the half darkness.

Beside the door Chip stopped and listened. He heard a stealthy rustle in the hay, heard a horse's rump thud against a stall and little Silver's distrustful snort. Someone was inside, no doubt of that. With a sudden impulse he bent and laid his rifle carefully on the ground close up against the stable wall, drew his six-shooter and, still stooping, slipped inside. Silver, he knew, was in the stall next the end, a pole fencing him in; whoever was down at that end couldn't see the doorway very well.

Standing in the blackness beside the door, he heard the brief scratching sound of a match. A small yellow glow followed, then the faint crackle of burning hay. There was a frightened trampling, the crack of a board as the colt lunged against the wall, and the hated snarl of Skelp Turner's vicious tones.

"Roast now—damn yuh! I wish t' hell I had yer owner tied in here with yuh, where you could all fry together!" There followed the clatter of a fork against the boards as Skelp snatched it up. "How'd yuh like a taste uh pitchfork, huh?"

The colt's agonized leap against the manger brought a cackle of glee from his tormentor. In the light of the small pile of burning hay Chip saw it all as he rushed forward.

"You drop that fork!" he thundered, and leveled his gun.

Skelp whirled, the three-pronged hay fork lifted like

a lance. "You, ay?" the wolfish grin as his lips drew back from yellowed teeth made his face scarce human. "I'll fork your liver into the fire!" he snarled. "I'll roast yuh like a rat in a haymow!" Animal courage of a sort he possessed, for he lunged straight at Chip in spite of the gun that roared almost in his face as he sprang.

The impact of the bullet threw him backward across the blaze. Chip dragged him writhing out of the flames and left him lying there, gasping foul threats and curses while he himself stamped out the fire.

With the light of a match he was standing tight-lipped beside the colt, examining the wounds in his sleek rump where three trickles of blood ran down, when suddenly the quiet night outside became clamorous with the roar of Harvey's shotgun and the instant reply of two rifles.

With a sidewise scrape of his foot he made sure that no smoldering sparks of the fire were left and started for the door. His foot struck against Skelp Turner, as limp and quiet now as he had been once before that night. Chip grunted an oath, groped in the dark for a moment, then picked him up and carried him outside the stable, where he dumped him unceremoniously and closed the door. Blood was high up on the man's chest and there was lots of it by the soggy feel of his clothes, but Chip had neither the time nor the mood now to see whether Skelp was dead or alive. Lest he revive to do further harm, Chip snatched Skelp's rope off his saddle there on the ground and trussed him hastily before dragging him over by the corral fence.

It seemed brutal—but he felt brutal when he thought of little Silver.

That done, he slipped over to the storehouse, keeping the building between himself and the house yard. After that first burst of shooting, quiet had fallen, and he was afraid the attackers were scattering. He did not want to run into them unexpectedly—and so he nearly did that very thing. For just as he was about to ooze around the corner of the building, a man spoke within four feet of him.

"I wish I knew who in hell put 'em wise!"

"Somebody sure did. That's a cinch. Wonder what—"

The crunch of footsteps and then Milt Cummings' cautious tones. "They've got the bulge on us, boys. Somebody blabbed, looks like." He swore with fluent viciousness.

"Well," another spoke impatiently, "what yuh go'na do, Milt? Back off and let 'em have the laugh?"

"Not on your life. They've got two men a'ready." He swore again, thickly, as if he had been drinking. "That sounded like Skelp Turner's shotgun. If I thought that old — had double-crossed me—"

"Yeah, but what you go'na *do?* Chew the rag till sun-up?"

"Aw, keep your shirt on, can't yuh? We're leavin' 'em think we're scared off fer a while. You two boys mosey down there in the field and touch a match to them haystacks. Make all the noise you can; might pick up a couple of the boys and take 'em along. If that don't bring them two — outa their holes, we'll burn the whole damn' works. If it wasn't for the women and kids, I'd do it anyway—"

"Yuh needn't git chicken-hearted over them women, Milt. That old battle-ax can sure take care of herself, and as for the little hell-cat of a Polly, I'd like nothin' better than to take her down a peg or two m'self. She—"

"You get goin' and fire them haystacks," Milt cut him off.

"Not much, you don't!" cried Chip, stepping around into sight. "Put up your hands—*empty!*"

It was a mad thing to do, with so many others within call, but he was beyond measuring chances. They heard the click of his gun and their hands went up as they whirled to face him. In the dim light they stared at him in silence, not knowing just how many of his friends might be just around the corner.

Chip thought of bluffing, but gave up the idea. Once he had bluffed and captured three men. But this was different. He couldn't make it work again like that. But he had to do something at once. Others might come, or one of the three might make a break, and if he fired a shot it would certainly raise hell. Let them once see he was alone . . .

"Walk straight up toward the house," he said curtly, "and keep your hands up." And when they hung back, "Don't think I won't shoot—"

"It's that damned Bennett kid!" Milt Cummings said bitterly. "He ain't with the Flying U, he's on his own. Throwed in with the rustlers." And suddenly he shouted, "This way, boys!" and threw himself to one side, firing from his hip as his hand swept downward.

"Take it, then," Chip muttered through his teeth, as he sent a shot at Milt, backing toward the corner.

Milt fired again, cursing Chip. From the house vague forms came running, shooting at random. One of the men with Milt gave a yell and collapsed against the rock wall. A bullet twitched Chip's hat as he ducked out of sight. From the woodpile the shotgun bellowed and a man running across the yard fell headlong, scrambled to his knees and sprawled again.

On his toes, Chip raced around the little building, rounded the third corner and ran head-on into a man who grunted and reached out to grab him. Chip swung his foot in a terrific kick, aimed a blow with his gun and heard the man grunt again, his arms jerking up, weakly clawing at the air. He went down and Chip turned the corner.

No one was there, but he heard steps behind him and raced for a hayrack, sitting on four rocks not far away. A bullet whined past his head as he ran and there was the crisp rattle of buckshot falling short of him on the frozen ground when the shotgun roared again. Evidently Harvey had lost all track of him and mistook him for a lyncher.

There was no way to show Harve who was fighting from the hayrack. Behind its shelter with his rifle laid across it, he began firing systematically at whatever moved out there in the dark. Whether he hit anyone he could not tell for certain, though dark formless shapes at which he fired sometimes seemed to waver as they merged into the shadows.

Up by the house the firing grew more continuous, as

though the attack was concentrating there and was being hotly defended. For a few minutes the shotgun bellowed frequently, then was silent. While he dodged from place to place behind that rack, shooting to confuse the aim of those who fired at his gun flashes, Chip had a thought to spare for Harvey, hoping he was all right.

Dodge as he would, a bullet found his scarcely healed left arm just above the elbow, numbing that hand until it was useless, at least for a time. So he left the rack, which was no real protection after all, and ducked back among the rocks at the base of a cliff wall and edged nearer to the stable corner. There he took shelter behind a boulder and prepared to fight it out with his six-shooter.

It bothered him that the shotgun by the woodpile had no more to say; but two rifles—old Shep and Snuffle Jones, he was sure—spoke their little pieces pretty regularly from the house, so he knew the lynchers were not getting inside. Nevertheless, he had an uncomfortable feeling that it could not go on much longer like this. Three against a crowd—they wouldn't come less than a dozen on their savage errand, and they were more likely to be twice that number, he thought. It would be hard to get into the house unless one of the men was hit. Harvey was out of it—dead, maybe; out of shells, perhaps. Out of the fight, that was a cinch. His own arm was bleeding a small, hot stream that dripped off his numbed fingers, and it seemed as though he couldn't hit anything he aimed at, any more. But he was keeping them away from the corrals, anyway. They'd have a sweet time trying to set anything afire so long as he could see to shoot.

Dizziness caught him just as he was standing up with some vague idea of going out into the open and offering to shoot it out with Milt. Storehouse, corral, even the dark hills began to revolve before his eyes. Spurts of flame out there showed double, and when he lifted his gun to shoot, it hung heavy from his hand. He took an uncertain step, saw the shadowy ground come up at him. So he sat down on it—to hold it still, he declared afterwards, though he knew all the while that the blood running down his arm was draining the strength from his body, and that if it didn't stop pretty darned soon, it would be all off with him.

How long he sat there, leaning against the boulder, he did not know. Two minutes or five—certainly not ten, the way he was bleeding. He had a hazy impression that the lynching party had for some reason separated, half of them climbing the hill back of the house and shooting down at the other half; vicious, stabbing spurts of fire which came nearer all the time. He didn't know what was the meaning of this new maneuver, but he saw the gun flashes and heard the *pow-w* of the shots.

Those down in the yard were backing up. Three or four blurred figures started running down the road—to their horses, he guessed. He wanted to hurry them up with a shot or two, but the effort didn't seem worth while after all.

And suddenly from the hillside there came a chorus

of yells that brought Chip up, clawing the rock to regain his feet, laughing foolishly all the while. The Happy Family with their own special war whoop were charging down upon the lynchers, coming miraculously out of nowhere. Happy Jack's raucous voice, fat old Slim's unmistakable bellow, Weary and Cal and Penny and Dickybird—their exultant tones rose and blended in a heavenly chorus. "Give it to 'em, boys! Pour it into them!" He thought he shouted that at the top of his voice, though no one seemed to hear him.

Down the last few feet of slope charged the boys of the Flying U, shooting as they ran. Before them, men scattered as chaff before a gust of wind, leaving choice strongholds (where they had settled for a siege that would end only when they could leave two men—or three, if they could get hold of Chip Bennett alive—dangling from the nearest tree) running like rabbits for farther coverts.

With a supreme effort, Chip steadied himself against the rock and sent one shot after the nearest, then settled back with a deep sigh of satisfaction. Let the boys clean up the rest, he thought vaguely. Couldn't cheat them out of their fun. . . .

Dreamily he was next aware of a lantern bobbing here and there about the yard, looking like a huge firefly. Taking tally, he guessed. It never occurred to him that he might be the object of their search. Let 'em hunt. He was too tired to care.

Then the lantern was shining in his face and all the boys were standing around, staring down at him.

Someone was holding him—that darned girl again! In the lantern light her eyes were big and shining. A drop of water fell on his nose, another on his cheek.

"You—took your time," Chip said in a washed-out tone.

"You're a nice one, getting that sore arm shot up again."

Her voice sounded queer; as if she were crying. That's where those drops came from, then. It wasn't rain, it was Polly Taylor crying. He wished she wouldn't. Nothing to cry about now, unless—

"Anything wrong—up at the house? Harve—"

"They're all right. Where's Skelp Turner?"

Skelp. That's right, he had forgotten all about Skelp. "Got him hog-tied—over by the fence. Tried to burn the stables." He sighed again wearily. Too much trouble to explain. No use, anyway. Let them go hunt up Skelp—find out for themselves. And he thought of little Silver with those three deep stabs in his hip. He had to go and wash them out with carbolic water. No telling what filth was on that fork. . . .

Struggling to rise, he was seized upon by Weary and Dick Bird.

"Let go. I'll pack him in," Dickybird's mild voice protested. "He's been bleedin' like a stuck pig. Got to stop it."

"I can walk. What's the matter with you fellows?" Chip tried to push them off with his one good arm, puzzled because the strength had seeped out of his body.

Then big Dick Bird gathered him up like a baby in

his long arms and went teetering on his little feet to the house, the lantern keeping pace beside him.

"I've got to—got to—"

"You ain't got to do nothin' but keep quiet," Dickybird cut him off.

"Little Silver. Skelp jabbed him with a pitchfork. I've got to—"

"Us boys'll look after that. We'll take care of the colt—and Skelp too." Bearing his burden of six feet of bone and muscle—and nerve—along, Dickybird's breathing was still even and unlabored.

"Skelp Turner, he's took care of a'ready," Slim announced, puffing up alongside. "Dead as a mackerel, by golly. Who done it? Chip, did you?"

"Sure as hell tried. Take care of the colt." And with that, soft blackness descended upon Chip.

XVI

CHIP STILL WANTS PROOF

SAVORY SMOKE FROM FRYING VENISON STEAKS ROSE to the low ceiling and hung there, mixing agreeably with the aroma of coffee, the warm wheaty smell of pancakes flavored with a dash of corn meal in the batter. Clatter of table things, the scuff of boot soles on the rough floor board, a voice now and then uttering a terse sentence. "More coffee, Mr. Whitmore?" . . . "Drive that cream pitcher this way." . . . "Who's got a corner on them pancakes?" . . . "Pass the butter, somebody." Yellow lamplight shining on tanned faces bent over filled plates. The quick light tread of the women moving from stove to table and back again.

Pancake turner in one hand, in the other a dish towel folded into a bunglesome makeshift holder, Polly Taylor pushed her slim body between Weary and Cal Emmett, leaned and drew in a long, deep breath; let it go with a rush over the lamp chimney. The flame jumped and went out. Acrid odor of burning oil wick scented the warm steamy air of the room. She shifted the towel to her shoulder and picked up the lamp.

"Morning," she announced succinctly. "I want to get those blankets off the window and let out a little of this smoke. It's thick enough to cut with a knife."

Eyes turned her way in wordless approval of her caution. Too sharp to uncover a window while the lamp was lit, even if there was a guard outside. Smart as the next one, that girl. Glances followed her as she walked in momentary gloom to a window, reached up and pulled a blanket off the two nails at the top of the sash, letting the heavy dark shield fall to the floor.

Filtered gray light enveloped her. Weary Davidson, who was nearest, straddled backward over the bench and went to help her where she stood struggling with a warped sash. As it went up, a keen, sweet breeze rushed in and set the breakfast smoke curling. From somewhere down near the stables two roosters were crowing a duet. A cow bawled down in the pasture.

Against the breeze Polly's check apron flapped, showing blue overalls beneath it and the .38 Colt swinging in its holster at her side. Strands of her copper red hair lifted on her temples and the shadows of weary sleeplessness beneath her fine eyes lay like splashes of purple paint.

She turned and looked back at the table filled with armed range men, her eyes seeking the one whiskered face in the group. "Can't I go out and tell those fellows to come in and eat, Pa? I'll stand guard till the rest of you are through."

"I'll go," Weary's quick tones intervened. "I'm full to the eyebrows. You stay inside. I guess we ain't reached the point yet where a girl's got to stand guard over us." His smile, sunny, even though his face was drawn and tired, robbed the words of any offense.

"Well, I'll go take a look at the patient then," Polly yielded in a carefully casual tone. "Maybe he can handle some breakfast." She drew in a long breath of fresh air and turned back toward the stove. "You watch the cakes, will you, Ma? They're about filled up, anyway." She referred to the dozen men around the table.

"Good thing they are," her mother made querulous retort. "If I hadn't been on the job, this whole griddle full would of been black as your hat. Go on with you. You better go to bed. I'll roust the boys out and make 'em wash the dishes." As Polly left the room, her mother's voice called after her, "He better not eat much. Something light. Ask him if he wouldn't like some milk toast. I can fix it in a minute—I've got the milk hot right here."

"All right, Ma. I'll ask."

But she didn't. She went first to the windows and raised the blinds and stood there looking out. From the wide, homemade couch in a corner, Chip turned his head and looked at her, conscious of the picture she made with the faint flush of early dawn lighting her face and her coppery hair lying in loose waves from crown to neck. It was the first time he had ever seen Polly Taylor without that big Stetson pulled down on her head. It had never occurred to him that her hair might be beautiful. Long silky lashes never impressed him much, possibly because women had raved about his own eyelashes as far back as he could remember—until he grew too big to stand for that kind of slush. But her profile as she stood there looking out into the coulee gave him an odd feeling of never having seen the girl before. Certainly he had never seen just that phase of Polly.

He wondered if it was just a crazy notion he had, that she had spilled tears on his face last night. She looked tired and worried and her shoulders drooped, as did the corners of her mouth, but she did not look as if she were at all likely to cry; certainly not over him or any other man. He guessed he kind of caved in, last night. Bullet in his arm. He remembered now. He was about all in when the boys showed up— And that was funny, their coming just in the nick of time. He wondered how they happened along; and then he knew. It was Polly, over there. Fogged over to the Flying U and notified the bunch. . . .

"How'd it pan out, last night?" he asked suddenly. "Anybody hurt on our side?" He lifted himself with an effort to his good elbow and balanced there, waiting for the room to quit spinning and settle down.

Polly turned and gave him a long enigmatic look. "Oh, no!" she said with much sarcasm. "Not at all. You came within an inch of bleeding to death, but of course that's nothing."

"Nothing at all." His tone closed the subject effectively. "I believe I asked how the fight turned out, but you needn't bother. If Weary's here, I'd like to see him, if it isn't too much trouble to ask. . . ."

Red flamed up into her face. She took a step toward him, storm in her eyes. "Oh, you—I'd like to slap you!"

"Yes?" The room refused to steady itself. Chip let himself down on the pillow again. "Go ahead. You have my permission." As his head cleared and the girl's figure ceased to waver like disturbed water in a pool, he saw that she was really trembling, glaring at him with her hands doubled into fists at her side. He honestly wondered why; he couldn't see what he had said or done that was so terrible. "When you get around to it," he said ironically, "would you mind asking Weary or—"

With a whispered word of suppressed fury, she turned and left the room, slamming the door after her so that the wail of an awakened baby rose within the next room.

Now that he was alone, Chip tried again to get up, with a little better success. He was sitting owlishly on the side of the couch when Weary came in with J.G., Shorty and old Shep Taylor behind him.

Weary set down a large milkpan in which a cup of coffee, two boiled eggs and a dish of milk toast were assembled. "How yuh feel, Chip? Mamma, you sure gave us a scare last night. Seems like you can't ever go into a fight without getting yourself all bunged up somehow. Throw this into you and maybe you'll feel better."

J.G. slumped into a nearby chair, hitching it closer to the couch. "If yuh feel like talkin', Chip, I wish you'd tell me just what you found out about all this business. You was down at Butch's place, the girl told us. He have any hand in the stealin'?"

Chip tasted the coffee, found it right and knew that Weary had probably sweetened it for him. "Not as far as I could find out. I was there a week, during the storm, and Butch was fine. I didn't take to the men he had with him, but I'm sure they didn't have any hand at all in the rustling."

"One of 'em was laid out cold last night," J.G. informed him flatly. "Feller they called Sime. Know 'im?"

"Sime?" Chip looked up so quickly it made his head whirl. "Sure, I know him. Rat, the way I sized him up," he said, when the vertigo passed. He dipped into the dish of eggs, trying to steady the shaking of his hand; gave it up and groped for his cigarette material, letting it go when Weary offered him a fresh-rolled smoke.

"You lay down and take it easy, old boy," Weary admonished. "You ain't in any shape to mix into this business now."

"We've got to get the straight of this," J.G. snubbed him. "I guess it won't kill him to talk a minute."

"Certainly I can talk. I'm not that far gone," Chip said peevishly, his face reddened with what blood was left in his lean body. He looked at Shep Taylor with some embarrassment. "You may as well get the fact that Butch and his men believed it was the Hobble-O doing the butchering. Butch as much as said so. He didn't want to get mixed up in it, but it looks like the jaspers he's got working for him were ready enough to take a hand in any little lynching that was going on. I don't believe Butch was here last night. He doesn't strike me as being that kind. It's the men he's got—"

"Poppycock!" snarled old Shep, with sudden violence. "You let 'im pull the wool over your eyes. Butch ain't no saint. He's in fer any devilment that's goin'. He knows damn well I ain't no rustler." He walked over to the fireplace and spat fiercely into the half-dead embers of last night's fire.

"Just the same, I don't believe he was here with that gang last night," Chip contended. And then he thought of something and turned white under his tan. "I'll damn soon find out," he declared, after a breathless pause, during which he was remembering how quickly Skelp Turner had softened toward him, when Chip spoke intimately of Big Butch and his men. "I'll make it my business to see where he stands. Soon as I'm on my feet again—"

Old Shep was raking the coals, laying on more wood, for the room was chilly. He turned with the long poker in his hand and strode to the couch. "Think I'm goin' to set around in the house and wait for you to scurrup around playin' deetectiff?" he demanded in his rasping voice. "I got work t'do. They'll be layin' in them hills tryin' to bushwhack us f'm now on till we git 'em cold."

J.G. gestured for silence. "What's all this about Milt Cummings being mixed up in it? Shep, here, says you told him you've got the goods on Milt, but you never told him how."

Chip had done a good deal of thinking on that subject. "I thought we could sweat it out of Skelp Turner," he confessed, "but by rights he oughta be dead. He is, if I can shoot worth a damn."

"Deader'n salt pork," Shorty gruffly attested. "How'd that happen, Chip? He was wrapped up in rope like a kid would tie a man. You do that?"

Chip colored again. "It was dark and the shooting had started up here at the house, and he'd played dead on me once before and crawled off in the dark to set the stable afire," he explained briefly. "I wasn't taking any more chance with him, that's all. I was pretty sure he was dead when I tied him."

"Mamma!" Weary murmured. "You sure are getting to be a real wolf!" He squatted on his heels beside the couch. "How'd Skelp get into the game in the first place?"

That much Chip told them. "But I haven't any proof except what Skelp said," he added dispiritedly. "I was going to jump Milt about it, but he was gone when I got to his place. I guess if he was honest, he might be just as liable to get a mob together and try and wipe out the Hobble-O."

"Not on your life," Weary grunted. "Milt plays

cinches. If he was honest, he'd wait and get the goods on the Hobble-O."

"I heard him down by the storehouse telling a couple of fellows to hustle down and burn the haystacks down in the coulee," Chip suddenly recalled. "He did say one thing that showed Skelp wasn't just talking through his hat. He threatened what all he'd do if Skelp had double-crossed him. Someone had blabbed, he said." He looked around the group. "I guess that shows plain enough Milt's the one."

J.G. got up, caught old Shep's eye and tilted his head toward the door. "That's good enough for me," he said, "and I guess it is for all of us. Milt's started this thing now and he's got to go through. Shorty, you go git the boys together. We've got to make a round-up here."

"Damn right there'll be a round-up," snarled old Shep as they went out.

Left alone, Chip tried to get up and follow. No use. His knees buckled under him and he lay back, cursing his luck. He looked at his bandaged arm that had put him down just when he needed to be at his best. Blood. He needed more of it in his veins to replace what had leaked out.

In the pan beside him the deep dish of milk toast stood cold and soggy. The eggs too were cold, and so was the coffee. No matter, his stomach wouldn't know the difference, maybe. Blood was made from food, wasn't it?

"Thank the Lord, I don't have to wait for a broken leg to mend," he muttered, and set himself doggedly to the task of swallowing everything in that pan except the dishes. And when he had finished, he lay down and as doggedly went to sleep. For he had a purpose to accomplish and his full strength was the one thing he needed.

XVII

FIGHT THE DEVIL WITH FIRE

WHILE CHIP LAY GLUMLY WAITING UNTIL THE HEALING forces of his body built new blood and fresh tissue—one for the whole length of him and the other for the bullet hole in his arm—events moved at what he considered a slow and uncertain pace. It must be that J.G. and Shep Taylor had lost their grip of things, he thought carpingly. They certainly didn't go after Milt and his crowd the way they should have done and so they made a flat fizzle of the whole thing.

Weary told him about it while the rest were eating supper that night. They had gone to Milt's place, the whole bunch of them, and they were ready for war. They had seen Milt all right—rode right up and called him to the door. Spike Reilly and Bill Hurst were there, monkeying with a bronc in the corral. Carl Jahn, another Lazy Ladder man, was laid out in the blacksmith shop, dead. They planned on burying him that afternoon, and a couple of the boys were up beyond the pasture, digging him a grave.

So that was the layout. "Milt talked straight," Weary sighed. "Setting there on my horse, listening to him, I couldn't see but what Milt was the injured party right from the word go. He claimed that all the evidence pointed straight to the Hobble-O, and he said he was so damned tired of being robbed that he made up his mind to make a clean-up. Claimed he still thought old Shep had stole about fifty head of beef from him. And he also made the claim that he's been losing calves right along, ever since Shep moved in here. Mamma, but he's a convincing cuss when he wants to be!"

Chip grunted. "Didn't anybody bone him about Skelp Turner, for the Lord sake?"

"Yeah, J.G. brought that up. Told him what Skelp had said. Milt, he offered to go out and choke the truth outa Skelp. Said he was a liar by the clock and had it in for him because he wouldn't have Skelp on the place." Weary shook his head. "I tell yuh, Chip, a feller can't help himself—he's got to believe Milt while Milt's talkin', anyway."

Chip turned himself impatiently on his bed. "Well, did you tell him what I heard last night? Heard him say—"

"Yeah—Cal busted out with that, way he always does horn in on any subject. Milt claims you got your lines crossed. He was cussin' Shep out and talkin' about Skelp at the same time, and you got things mixed. Milt says he thought he knowed the sound of Skelp's shotgun, and he thought mebby Skelp had been snoopin' around, gettin' an earful, and was trying to get a whack at 'em just for devilment. Milt said it would be just Skelp's idea of a joke to stand 'em off at the Hobble-O, and down Milt if he could, and then turn around and kill old Shep himself, and let on like it was all done in the fight. That's all he had in mind, he said, and you got the wrong idea. He says him and Skelp Turner have been on the outs for the last two years and more, and he's had to ride with one eye peeled for the old cuss whenever he was over in Skelp's part of the country."

"And you damned chumps swallowed that?"

"Well, I didn't myself—I don't know about the rest. But it did kinda ball things up some. You can't," sighed Weary, "just take a man out and hang him, unless you've got his guilt cinched on him so tight he can't crawl out of it." He licked his cigarette down and twisted the ends, meditating upon the statement. "You can't, unless you're the strangler type yourself and kinda take to the job natural," he amended, while he hunted for a match.

He gave Chip the cigarette, lighted it for him and began making another for himself.

"I could," Chip said savagely. "Milt, anyway." He blew a mouthful of smoke and gave a characteristic snort. "He's guilty as hell and you know it."

"I expect he is, all right. But this was a bright sunny morning. Anyway, Milt put up a damned good argument, Chip. If I didn't know you like I do, darned if I wouldn't of taken his word for it." He looked at Chip. "Skelp Turner was a skunk," he said tentatively.

"Sure he was. He also thought I was one of the gang and talked accordingly. If you want to think Milt Cummings is a little tin angel, go to it—"

"Aw, come off your perch. I don't think nothing like that. I used to, but not any more. None of us do.

Shep's going up around Milk River—starts in the morning—and pick up a bunch of riders that'll put the fear of the Lord into that Lazy Ladder outfit, if they so much as wall an eye toward the Hobble-O. We kinda ride herd around here till he gets back."

He turned his head, listening to the supper sounds in the next room. He tossed his half-smoked cigarette into the fire and yawned. "I sure do hope I don't have to leave the bed-ground tonight," he said. "They know we're on the job so I guess they'll ride the other side of the crick tonight. They know damn well they got off cheap, losin' only Carl Jahn. If it had been Spike, now—"

"The last card isn't turned yet," Chip muttered.

Weary stood up, yawned again. Thirty-six hours, most of them in the saddle, had taken toll of him. "Well, they'll be bringin' in a hot mash for yuh, any time now," he observed. "How's the arm, anyway?"

"Not so worse." Chip bit his lip. "I'll be outa here in another day."

Weary grinned skeptically. "Not if Polly's rope don't bust, you won't. Boy, you're sure goin' to convalesce accordin' to Hoyle this time."

"I'm damned if I do!" snapped Chip. But Weary only grinned the wider.

"You got things to learn about Polly," he stated darkly, as he went out.

Calm days of sunshine followed and Weary was very nearly right, at least where Polly was concerned. So many riders ranging about made it plainly unnecessary for her to be riding from dawn to dark, and

Chip saw Polly in checked gingham and flowered calico, with her sleeves rolled up most of the time, showing unsuspected dimples in her elbows. Also the untaught waves in her copper-red hair disturbed him, especially when she stooped to smooth his pillow or to bring him food. But he would have died before he admitted it, and that gave him a sullen look when she was in the room and made his manner toward her aloof, with a frigid politeness that almost drove Polly to man-sized cusswords.

But there was plenty of work to keep her elsewhere. There were the children, with their incessant demands and their fiercely sudden quarrels to arbitrate. There was the cooking for hungry riders who came and went. There was the boot-tracked kitchen to scrub every day or two, and the baby to hush, while her mother snatched a little rest or did the more expert baking.

Four full days of that, while Chip forced himself to lie as quiet as the scabbarded rifles on the saddles of the Flying U boys. It irked him terribly that not a gun smoked during all that time. They were letting Milt Cummings get away with it and he called them fools and worse. Milt was just holing up like a coyote, waiting until things quieted down. He'd get old Shep where the hair was short and it would just serve the old fool right. Milt was nobody's fool. He proved that when he soft-soaped J.G. into thinking he was a hell of a fine feller that just lost his temper and made a pass at hanging some of his neighbors before he cooled off. That was what it all amounted to, the way Milt talked.

Chip held his impatience in with as tight a rein as if it were a horse that kept trying to bolt. He couldn't afford to crowd that cussed arm right now. Start that vein, or whatever it was, to leaking again, and he might just as well cut his throat and make a quicker job of it. He did not fool himself. He had come as near bleeding to death as was comfortable, and like it or not, he had to take it easy for a while.

Fortunately, the bullet wound was a clean puncture, that had missed the bone, and healthy flesh heals quickly. Polly's mother had learned a good deal about bullet wounds in her years on the frontier and with rare common sense she did the necessary things and left Nature to attend to the rest. So, while it seemed a terribly long while to Chip, strength flowed swiftly back into his flaccid muscles, no doubt speeded by his indomitable will to be back at his job.

On the fifth day after the fight, several incidents marked a change at the Hobble-O. Early that morning, the Happy Family rode with J.G. back to the Flying U, openly expecting Chip to follow as soon as he was able to ride. Chip felt able to ride whenever he chose, but he lay quiet until they were well away from the ranch.

Late the night before, old Shep had returned from up Harve way. Half a dozen wire-muscled men with the brown faces of riders had unrolled their blankets in the Hobble-O bunkhouse. Real go-getters by the look of them, Weary reported to Chip, when he said good-bye in the morning. Three of them packed 30-30's, two had long-barreled 45-70's—he didn't get a chance to see what the sixth man carried; a carbine of some sort. Anyway, they'd be hard customers to go up against, and he guessed the Hobble-O wouldn't need to call on the neighbors again to help 'em out.

That being the case, Chip turned again to his own affairs. When the ranch was quiet and even the two boys had climbed the coulee wall on some mysterious business of their own, Chip drew his bandaged arm out of its sling and worked it carefully into his sour-dough coat. He pulled on his chaps and buckled on his spurs and his gun and took his rifle from the corner where Polly had stood it the day after the fight—she having cleaned it with meticulous care.

He told the surprised Mrs. Taylor that he was going for a ride and he didn't know when he might be back, but he was mighty grateful for all she had done for him, and his arm was all right now. As an afterthought, he asked her if she would tell Shep he'd like to leave his colt there for a while.

"You be careful you don't start that arm bleeding again," she admonished him, hushing the baby cuddled over her shoulder. "I'll tell Shep, but it don't matter, anyway. Anything you want on this ranch is yours and you know it. Or you ought to. We don't forget a kindness here—nor a wrong, either."

"Same here," Chip declared, with one of his rare smiles. "I certainly won't forget the way you took care of this arm of mine, and—"

"Well, I hope I don't have it all to do over again," she broke in, with a brusqueness that would deceive no one. "You be careful; that's all I got to say. You going back to work for the Flyin' U again?"

Chip reddened. "Well, I—I've got a little something to do first—" It was difficult to lie to a person like Lavina Taylor, more difficult still to parry that direct and piercing gaze which she sometimes employed. "I—"

"When you get outside this coulee, you better have eyes in the back of your head," she stated surprisingly, one red-knuckled hand patting the baby with a mechanically soothing motion. "No use tryin' to talk you out of it, I guess—you're about as stubborn as they make 'em. But remember one thing, Chip. If there ain't a bounty on your scalp right now, there will be. I wish you'd stay quiet till that arm's well."

"It's well enough." His mouth had pinched in at the corners. "I'll take care of my scalp, all right."

"Well, I'd hate to see—" Her voice trailed into silence. Her eyes clouded, looking back along the dim years to other bold young fellows who had made that boast—and failed to keep it, some of them. "They all know how it was we had warnin' in time," she said. "They've got that chalked up against you and don't you forget it." Her breath sucked in with a sibilant sound, as if a sudden pain had caught her. "You're goin' after Milt yourself—now, ain't yuh?"

Chip gave her a startled glance. "What makes you think that, Mrs. Taylor?"

"I don't think it. I know it. And I want to give you a word of advice." She hesitated. "You never fought Injuns—but you've heard tell of how cunning they are. You're going up against them that's worse than Injuns. More treacherous. Recollect, Milt Cummings has passed as a nice fellow and a nice neighbor. He's married into the Cow Island clique. The way he's worked his scheme to get two honest men hung for his own devilment—Daniel in the lion's den had a cinch compared to what you're starting out to do."

"I know that. But I'm planning to live in this country and I'm not going to spend the rest of my life dodging bullets. The only way to clean up this business is to dig up proof that'd stand in court. Milt's making me out a liar and that's something I don't stand for a holy minute." As his hot angry eyes met hers, he forced a smile that seemed to beg her pardon for his boasting. "When I lie down it'll be for a bullet," he explained, a boyish diffidence overtaking him. "It won't be because I've quit." And he added, "All anybody can do is try."

"Well, I only hope and pray you succeed," sighed Polly's mother. "I know Shep's life ain't safe, and it won't be, till that bunch is cleaned out. And if I was a man, Chip, I'd look at it the way you do." She turned abruptly and set the baby down on the floor, heedless of his resentful squall. "You won't feel much like cookin' for a day or two and chances is it won't be any too safe to show a fire. You wait a minute and I'll put you up a meal or two of grub."

"What I want most," Chip found courage to say, "is a couple of those cowhides stacked in the shed."

"My land, take all yuh want," she called from the pantry. "Fight the devil with fire, is what I always say."

Chip's spirits lifted. Polly's mother was a brick; not a bit like that darned daughter of hers. With a flour sack half filled with fresh-baked bread and a couple of pies and plenty of doughnuts, he went stilting down to the corrals in his high-heeled boots. The friendly admonitions of Polly's mother warmed his heart and put a glow of optimism in his purpose.

With his hat tilted over one eyebrow, his gun riding snug at his hip and his big-roweled spurs making pleasant clinking sounds against the stirrups, he rode away down the coulee with Jeff well packed and following amiably at Mike's heels. His back was straight and his chin was stubborn, and he didn't give a darn if he met Polly Taylor square in the road. He'd show her, by thunder, that he was his own boss and would do as he pleased. He wasn't broke to the halter yet, he'd tell her. He didn't lead worth a cent.

XVIII

THE WIND'S IN THE NORTH

IN A HIDDEN LITTLE POCKET IN THE HILLS CHIP SPENT nearly the whole afternoon fashioning eight crude but satisfactory boots of the cowhides begged from Mrs. Taylor, and in helping the two horses accustom themselves to the feel of the awkward things on their feet. When Mike quit kicking and with a final disgusted snort resigned himself to the indignity, Chip mounted and rode on, following a carefully thought-out plan he had made while he lay apparently dozing in his bed at the Taylor's.

That night he camped in the Devil's Dipper, with a rope stretched across the six-foot entrance, and the certainty that no one could ever trail him to the spot. Regardless of Polly's slighting remarks about the place, he considered it as good a hide-out camp as he could expect to find; at least, for the time being.

Daybreak next morning found him away over in the canyon that led by devious windings to the eastward valley, riding slowly and scanning every inch of the ground, as he neared the rocky gorge down which his trailer the other day must have gone. Now that he knew the kind of mark those cowhide boots left behind them, tracking was possible wherever a hoof would leave a print. There were faint impressions to be seen even where the ground was hard, and in the softer soil were blurred shapeless tracks that resembled hoofprints months old. It was no wonder he had failed to trace the killers in his first week and more of hunting this broken country; but it angered him now to think how he had been fooled.

With their trick known, he read aright certain vague impressions in a dry wash branching off from the southern side of the canyon, just before it narrowed to the bottle-neck gorge. The mild and windless days since these marks were made had not blown the sand, and the prints remained as they had been that day. By looking back and studying Mike's muffled tracks, he could tell just what marks to look for ahead of him. His lip curled. Smart, weren't they? But they hadn't been smart enough to pick up that boot when it dropped off a horse's foot. They had left it by a sagebrush to give their show away. So now it was a snap.

As he rode on and on, turning and twisting amongst the network of narrow gulches and draws that seamed the butte's ragged base, he saw many marks such as Mike was making; so many, that without Mike's tracks before his eyes as a sample, he would have thought the marks were made by the freakish gouging of vagrant winds. Now he knew better. He knew he had struck the trail where the Lazy Ladder men rode across to the northern part of the breaks to do their stealing.

A rough and difficult trail it was in spots, with steep pitches in and out of pinched gullies. No one would ever dream of looking for a trail through here. There were places where his stirrups touched the rock on either side and he had to turn his knees in against his horse to avoid scraping them. Certainly no packed horses ever came through this way. Chip saw very clearly why the stolen beef was taken around the other side of the butte to Skelp Turner's camp.

Simple! So simple that when he arrived suddenly at a distinct fork in the vague trail he was following, the significance of the circumstances at first did not occur to him. A divided opinion about a bad bit just ahead, he thought it, and chose the right-hand gulch for no particular reason except perhaps that Mike showed interest in that direction, walking with springy knees of expectancy, ears tilted forward. There was no mistaking that attitude. Chip swung off where a splinter of rock offered some concealment for his horse and went forward to investigate afoot.

Not following the blurred trail, however. Instead, he climbed a tilted seam along the rock wall—for he had no intention of meeting some of the Lazy Ladder gang face to face in that narrow place. True, they might shoot him off the side where he couldn't very well hide himself, but he counted on not being discovered. Men with wide-brimmed hats bend their glances toward the ground, as they ride, or look out at a level, as a rule. Unless they heard him, they would not be likely to look up. And furthermore, the broken seam kept climbing, fairly easy to follow. Another minute or so and he was up above a bulging out-thrust which would hide him from anyone on the ground. And still he heard no one approach.

Then, looking always ahead, he glimpsed trees and knew that the gulch must end in an open space. Perhaps some secret basin where something might be learned. He went on. And he heard a man shout some phrase of greeting. Though the words did not reach him, he could tell by the tone.

Unexpectedly he was facing a valley which looked vaguely familiar. Below him rose the smoke from a cabin chimney, and a corral fence swung out from the cliff. Men were talking, immediately beneath him, and in the windless air of midmorning their words came to him with a disquieting clearness.

Big Butch was one and he was asking some strange man what kind of a trip he had had. The stranger said it was all right, and the boys were at the river and would be drifting in that night.

"Didn't know as we better head this way all in a

bunch," he explained. "We heard about the fizzle the other night—"

They talked of the fight at the Hobble-O and another voice joined in, then another. Voices Chip knew, talking in a way that set the blood pounding in his veins.

With a slow careful movement, he reached up and pulled off his hat, afraid that some one might chance to look up and get a glimpse of it. On his belly he inched forward to the very edge, hoping for a sight of the speakers; but all he saw was a black hat, set far back on a head and hiding it completely, and a pair of shoulders drooped forward; some one roosting on the corral fence, he knew by the posture. The stable roof, jutting out, hid all the others from his sight. Probably, he thought, they were hunkered down on their boot heels against the stable wall, smoking while they talked, as range men have a fashion of doing.

"I hear they got Sime."

"Yeah, the damn fool didn't have sense enough to crawl into his hole," Butch's voice answered. "I told him to keep his nose out—"

"Flicker, he picked up a bullet, too, some one was tellin' me."

"Not that night, he didn't. Flicker was home in bed when that jamboree was goin' on. I've been side-steppin' this cattle stuff, much as I could."

"Milt, he kinda overplayed his hand, looks like to me," another voice spoke carpingly. "Why'n hell didn't he wait a week or so, before he opened up the ball?"

Butch's voice was explanatory. "Well, for one thing, the weather turned off warm all of a sudden and the butcherin' had to stop—unless they wanted to pitch good beef into a gully somewhere. The boys made a big killin' and done that a coupla times, but Milt, he don't go very strong on that kinda work. Milt hates like hell to see a dime git away from him. Then . . ."

"Thought he was goin' to ring the Flyin' U in on it and make—"

"Seems like they wouldn't ring . . ."

A pulse in Chip's throat started hammering so hard it almost choked him while he listened. They talked about Milt, criticizing him behind his back and naming his faults and his weaknesses. They drifted into intimate and terribly revealing talk of their own plans and how they meant to carry them out. They discussed old Shep Taylor as if he were a man already dead, and seemed to know a surprising lot about his ranch, his family and his affairs. They knew the names of the men he had hired up Milk River way, and their general characteristics. There was one, Blink Roberts, whose presence at the Hobble-O seemed to furnish them with a good deal of amusement. They said, over and over, leave it to Blink.

They talked of the Flying U. . . .

Until Sam's raucous voice called them in to their dinner, Chip lay up there among the rock rubble and listened, eyes fixed with a terrible intentness upon that black hat and the bowed shoulders beneath. Once his hand reached back and closed upon the butt of his gun, then loosened and came away, as sober sense warned him that this was not the time. He did not know whose head that hat covered, nor did he identify any particular voice with the wearer; but an occasional outflung hand told him when that man was speaking and the temptation to end his speech with a leaden period was almost irresistible at times.

But to kill the man in the black hat would have accomplished nothing except to bring them all like hounds on his trail, and that he could not afford. Not now. Not now, while all their desultory talk, so self-revealing, and all the plans they had discussed together was locked away in his memory. Risk enough now that a bullet might blot out the knowledge he carried before he could make use of it. Milt and Milt's men were hunting him—or they would be, as soon as they discovered he had left the Hobble-O. "—and damn it, I keep tellin' Milt that Chip Bennett's only one white chip in this game—" While Chip lay up here, fingering his six-shooter, they had all laughed at Butch's pun. But it was true, nevertheless. In this game he was just a white chip—and yet, sometimes a white chip may win or lose the game.

No, he couldn't take a chance more than he had to now. Lucky for him he had borrowed their trick of muffling their horses' feet, he thought, as he made his way cautiously back down to where Mike stood. If they used this secret trail—as they no doubt would sooner or later—they would see no strange tracks. It might, he thought, be an advantage sometime to know this back way in to Fishback Canyon, as Butch called his place.

Riding back the way he had come, at the fork in the trail he paused just long enough to note the other trail's direction. The trail over to the Lazy Ladder, he was now certain. And he rode half turned in the saddle after that, watching back the way he had come, feeling his back muscles relax whenever he turned a bend and knew a bullet could not follow him there.

But the winding way lay empty to the noon sun. The canyon was still with that breathless silence of a barren land, lying forsaken by men. As quickly as he could, he got back into the Devil's Dipper where he could feel secure. Yet even here he was suspicious and uneasy, almost certain some one had been there in his absence. Some things were moved in his makeshift camp, the rope across the entrance tied with a different knot.

With his rifle close at hand and his glance straying often to that crevice through the ridge which was the only means of getting to him, he ate a little and rolled a cigarette and thought of his next move.

It wasn't easy to decide. Sometimes his thoughts reeled round and round, the different diabolical things he had heard that day weaving drunkenly together, darting thoughts flying from one to another like a swarm of midges that never alighted anywhere. And he had to do some straight, hard thinking. Those devils back there—it was up to him whether they made a go of their plans.

Chip never dreamed how thin and drawn his face looked, nor how his eyes were sunken in their sockets and gleamed with pin-point pupils, as he sat there on his bed roll, staring down the rocky handle of the Devil's Dipper, his rifle laid across his knees while he tried to smoke and relax, so that he could think things out and decide just what he ought to do first. Relax!—While his wounded arm ached like a throbbing tooth and his whole body cried out for rest; and the cigarette he had started to smoke went cold in his tense fingers, and the consciousness of being hunted glued his gaze to the one vulnerable point in his retreat.

But after a little, one thought detached itself from the spinning confusion. Haste! What he had to do, he must do quickly, before the Lazy Ladder stopped him with a bullet. After that, it didn't matter very much. If they got him, he thought moodily, they wouldn't get much; not after he had told what he knew. But he had that one job to do first. He had to get out of here and tell. He *had* to.

That much then was clear in his mind now and it brought a certain release from the strain. The horror of his knowledge was passing, settling into a determination to give those devils back there a surprise. There was only one way to do that and the job was his. If he weren't man enough to put it over . . .

Mechanically his shoulders lifted in a shrug at that contingency, and the movement had an odd effect of throwing off the spell of confused dismay at what he had learned. He looked at his cigarette, tossed it into the ashes of his breakfast fire and made himself a fresh one, being particular to tear off a strip of paper of the exact width he preferred.

"And I hope I get a chance to tell Butch he better not

talk so loud next time," he muttered grimly as he snapped the tiny paper pellet into the dead fire. "He sure as hell stuck his head in the noose that time—and I hope I can tell him so before he steps off on nothing. Give me a job breaking broncs! Huh!"

Now he smoked quietly, satisfyingly, drawing long meditative breaths through the little brown cylinder. The lines around the taut bow of his lips eased perceptibly. He got up, broke small sage twigs and stacked them precisely in the exact center of his placed rocks in the ashes, held a match flame steadily beneath a handful of frayed bark under the twigs, set other sticks, one by one, crisscross on the blaze that leaped and spread. He carried his coffeepot to the spring, emptied it and rinsed it well and half filled in with water. While it was heating, the pot balanced nicely upon two rocks over the fire, he got out his battered little coffee mill, filled the hopper full of the roasted beans and ground vigorously with his good right arm, the mill gripped between his knees. Twice as much as he usually ground for himself alone, but he wanted the brew double strength today.

There was need of haste, of course, and yet there was time enough to rest for an hour, he knew. In the face of his inner urge to hurry, hurry, he forced himself to take this hour quietly, letting Mike graze at will. They both needed the rest. Moreover, he had gathered that "big medicine" was to be made that afternoon at Butch's place. Milt and all his men would probably be there, working out details of their plan. This afternoon his only danger lay in some lone sniper set to watch for him—and even a Lazy Ladder man could only be in one place at a time. He wouldn't look for Chip Bennett away down in here. And as for the fancied meddling with his outfit—well, that was probably some of that darned Polly Taylor's work. It would be kinda funny if she didn't come nosing around, looking for him. He never saw such a girl.

Yet his eyes brightened in spite of him when he met her as he emerged into the main canyon and was stopping on a patch of shale rock to take the cowhide off the horses' feet. She rode up and sat looking down at him in disapproving silence, while he tied the pieces of hide under the canvas on Jeff's pack.

"I suppose," she said at last, "you think you're being smart. scurruping off like this with that arm of yours."

From under his gray hatbrim Chip looked up at her. "I couldn't very well scurrup off without it, could I?"

"You didn't have to scurrup at all," Polly retorted, pinching a smile in at the corners of her red mouth. "I'd like to know what you think you're doing, away off down here."

"Yes? I rather suspected as much." Chip's smile was calculated to infuriate her and it almost succeeded.

"Sometime," she observed darkly, "I think I shall have to choke you, or brain you with an ax, or put strychnine in your pancake batter, or something."

"The ax, please," Chip made his choice unmoved; "and be darned sure you make a good job of it or I'm liable to resent it."

"You'll stay where you belong, if I ever start in on you," she promised. And then her tone changed as he finished and swung up on Mike, reining in alongside her. "Been taking a leaf out of Milt Cummings' book, I see. I hope you found out all you wanted to know?"

"Certainly. I usually do, don't I?"

"Depends on how much you want to know." And suddenly she shivered exaggeratedly. "I do wish the wind would change out of the north," she complained. "I've been frozen for a month."

Chip gave her a quick surprised glance before he understood. It was a hint for him to thaw out, but perversely he would not take the hint. If she wouldn't butt into his affairs all the time, maybe he . . .

"Pa wants you to come straight on back," she told him, breaking into his thoughts. "He says you'll get yourself killed, if you don't look out, riding around in these breaks the way you do, with a hundred chances to pot-shot you."

"And how about yourself? I should think your dad would tie you up if you can't be kept on the ranch any other way." He looked at her, frowning. "You're taking long chances, if you only knew it."

"Not as long as you take. Milt wouldn't bother me and you know yourself that Butch wouldn't let anybody touch me." She drew in her breath, looking at him queerly. "His bunch is back from driving those horses south," she said. "At least, Snuffle came in from Cow Island and said they were all ganged in at Lang's, drinking and gambling. A dozen or more strangers, he said, besides the men that were here all winter. Looks like he means to do a land-office business, breaking horses to sell. Are you going to work for him?"

"That," said Chip, "remains to be seen." It was on the tip of his tongue to tell Polly something of what he had heard; as if it might be safer to pass on what he knew to the first person he saw.

But he did not, and for a reason he could not quite understand. He did not want to worry Polly. Stealing sidelong glances at her, as they rode side by side, he felt an odd desire to keep trouble and worry far from her; keep her saucy and smiling and courageous and never let her guess what terrible knowledge was in his mind.

"Besides," Polly said irrelevantly, breaking the silence between them, "Dad said if I had any idea whereabouts to find you, I'd better bring you in. He said Milt had men on the prowl, and you'd get in safe, as long as I was with you."

Her tone challenged him to biting resentment, but in that moment Chip was only conscious of old Shep's shrewdness and was grateful.

"Well, if you're appointed bodyguard," he said dryly, "better shake that cayuse of yours up a little. The sooner we get in, the better I'll be pleased."

And Polly could only look at him in blank amazement, wondering what had come over him.

But Chip knew. For the next few hours his life, as he saw it, was about the most precious thing north of the river and it had to be preserved. After tonight—well, he'd stack up just about as high as any other bone-headed cowpuncher, he guessed, and if somebody put his light out, he wouldn't be greatly missed.

XIX

"IT'S LIFE AND DEATH, POLLY"

SUPPER WAS READY IN THE TAYLORS' BIG KITCHEN, and Polly in her overalls, and with her hair braided down her back, was taking up fried eggs expertly with a thin old table knife and cuddling them into all the spaces and hollows on a huge platter of fried ham. From under his straight dark brows Chip watched her, without seeming to do so, and snubbed her with a frigid politeness when she brought the platter first to his elbow. And for that, Polly deliberately spilled a drop or two of boiling hot coffee on his hand when she later made the rounds, refilling empty cups. The revenge was robbed of its sweetness, however, when Chip refused to flinch or to move so much as a finger. And from this, one may gather that their relations were perfectly normal and Chip was himself again.

Along the kitchen wall, behind the door, eight rifles leaned, chambers loaded and with the magazines full as they would hold. The ninth, which belonged to Chip, stood behind the door in the living room. And that was for a reason which he kept to himself.

He was the first one through. As he pushed back the stool which served for the end of the table—his place by the authority of Polly's mother, she having a care for his sore arm—his glance traveled swiftly down the line of heavy, absorbed, feeding faces bent over their plates. Unlike the boys of the Flying U, these men ate without speech, minds wholly concentrated upon the food before them. His lip curled a little at the animal display of them as he stood there fumbling a pocket for his smoking material.

He was playing for time until he could meet old Shep's eye. But Shep was hungry after a full day in the saddle and he was busy. Chip turned away, passed close to Polly and gave her a deliberate nudge. Polly almost dropped the plate of piled biscuits she was carrying to the table, she was so surprised. "Come to me," said Chip's eyes when she looked up at him, and he went on into the other room.

Within two minutes she was there, breathing a little fast, a flush in her cheeks and starry question in her eyes. She stood with her back against the door and looked at Chip, where he leaned against the fireplace, rolling a smoke. "Well?"

Chip drew a match across a jutting rock, held the blaze up where it cast a flickering glow on his thin dark face. "Can you get your dad in here without stampeding that bunch of longhorns out there?" In spite of himself, his voice hinted at dark things untold.

"Why, of course!" She left the door and came swiftly toward him. "They aren't so wild as all that." She stood before him, watching him light his cigarette. "You did find out something down there. What did you find out?"

"Plenty. Go get your dad before he goes out. He came in so late I didn't have a chance—"

"He's just started on his pie. He'll fill his pipe before

he gets up from the table. He always waits and smokes till Ma's through eating. I'll tell him then. What did you find out?"

Chip looked down at her, his eyes softening. "Nothing to worry you about—" And he caught himself on the verge of tenderness, "—and curiosity killed the cat, remember."

"Oh! Of all the mean, despisable—" She stamped a foot.

"Yes, I know that song by heart. Trot along and do as you're told, why don't you?"

"I won't!" But she retracted that. "If it wasn't important, maybe, I wouldn't go a step."

"But it is important. It's life and death." It was a slip and his look proved it.

"And you won't tell me?"

"No."

"It seems," she said bitterly, "that I haven't earned your confidence—or any consideration even."

His face whitened a little. "You know better than that. This is a—it's something for your father and J.G. to settle. I've no right to tell anybody but them. I—it's too—it goes away beyond you and me, Polly. We don't cut any ice at all. I wish you'd go get your dad. He can do his smoking in here, for once." He looked at her so that she turned her eyes away. "This isn't a time to squabble over words," he said almost gently. "After I've done what I've got to do—I'll tell you the whole thing."

She gave him one long look, turned and left the room without a word.

Old Shep came, cuddling the bowl of his pipe, his eyes two boring questions. And, "What you got on your chest?" he demanded. "Know anything new?"

"Yes. You and I are going to ride over to the Flying U tonight. I'll take my outfit along and leave it there. I won't be needing it any more, I guess."

Old Shep took his pipe from his mouth, held his whiskers out of the way and spat into the fire. "What'n hell's happened?"

"Nothing—yet. Tell Snuffle you'll be back tomorrow, and one man on guard will be enough tonight. Or none at all. Let them think everything's riding along about the same."

"Ain't it?" Shep stabbed the question into Chip's measured speech.

"Just about, only I don't think there'll be any trouble for a day or two. And say, take Blink Roberts along with you. Make any excuse you want to—but take him along and don't let him know where we're headed for."

"Dammit, I don't make excuses to my men," snapped Shep.

"Suit yourself. That's up to you." Chip rubbed out his cigarette against the rock and flipped the stub into the blaze. "Better take Blink on some errand with you, and I'll come along and ask which way you're riding, and invite myself along, as far as you happen to be going my way." His cheeks darkened as the blood rushed in. "I don't go much on private theatricals," he added, "but not knowing just who might be up on the rim, or—" he flung out a hand "—just how the cards lie here, it's best to make the play natural and not excite anybody's curiosity."

Shep drew a long breath through his pipe. "Why yuh want that feller Blink Roberts in pa'ticular?"

"Well, he's a good man to have along, isn't he?"

"S'posed t' be. Come an' boned me for a job and give a good account of hisself, so I hired him."

"Well, take him. I—I want him along, that's all."

Shep eyed him thoughtfully. "Any reason why yuh can't spill what yuh know?"

Chip shook his head. "Only, it's a long story and I want you and J.G. to hear it together." He glanced out the window. "We ought to get started before dark," he said. "We don't want this to look mysterious to anybody that might be interested."

He had thought this all out, weighing and declining during the long ride in with Polly. Now he was aware of Shep's disapproval—almost his disgust at being asked to make foolish mystery and go riding off without knowing why. He couldn't blame Shep if he refused to stir away from the ranch without knowing why. Almost he was tempted to tell what he knew; almost. But there was the danger that Shep would want to act alone, go off half-cocked with his seven men. . . .

Shep grunted and swore and deluged the feebly burning juniper roots. But he did not finish his pipe before he was gone from the room and telling his wife she could look for him back sometime tomorrow, for he was going on up to the Flying U and she was not to peddle the information to any one, not even Snuffle.

The play went forward as Chip had planned it. He let the two ride off while he was fussing with his pack, then trotted his horses to overtake them, while they were still in the coulee. He thought that Blink Roberts looked curious and even a little perturbed, and he caught the man glancing up at the eastern rim more often than any save a frightened man would do, or one who had a special interest in the spot. But no signal was attempted—indeed there was nothing Blink could possibly know that would be of immediate interest to any watching enemy, except perhaps the fact that Chip Bennett was riding off with his pack horse and his pet colt; and that any man on the rim could see for himself.

It was a touchy half mile and Chip was glad the shadows lay so dark beneath the hill and that the willows along the creek blurred the outlines of any riders along the trail. Until he caught the upward glances of Blink, he hadn't realized how fine a target he would make nor the risk he would run. But it seemed that the rim was for the time being clear of spies. At any rate, they left the coulee and turned into the Whoop-up Trail going north, and no bullet came seeking him out.

There on the level the fading glow of sunset gave a stronger light and he could study the man they called Blink Roberts. An unobtrusive type; at the table an hour ago, Chip had tried to guess which man among the strangers was Blink Roberts and never guessed that this was he. Sandy-haired, with a roundish face reddened by riding all day in the sun, and a pair of mild, light blue eyes and a reddish mustache. He looked, Chip thought, like a nester who would keep a dirty stable and raise a swarm of kids, with a wife who always put too much saleratus in her biscuits. As he rode beside old Shep, his stiffened legs thrust his stirrups out forward and they lifted and fell with the motions of his horse. Limber Chip Bennett, graceful as a young Indian in the saddle, curled his lip at such awkwardness.

But two guns were holstered on Blink's full cartridge belt and the stock of his rifle sticking out of its scabbard under his stirrup fender showed the marks of use. He chewed tobacco with a slow, deliberate working of his jaws and winked his light eyelashes every time his teeth clamped down. He seemed to have a great capacity for silence, for he never spoke a word or betrayed any interest whatever in the journey. He just chewed and spat neatly off to the side, and rode along, keeping his thoughts—if he had any—to himself.

A stolid, harmless type except in a fight, to look at him. But there was his name, spoken familiarly in that group by Big Butch's stable, and there was the statement that they could leave it to Blink. Leave what to Blink? The killing of Chip Bennett? But Big Butch liked him, Chip knew. He hadn't spoken so enthusiastically of Milt's grudge. Leave Blink to some treachery of his own, the giving of information perhaps?

Whatever it was, Chip was not sorry that Jeff and little Silver gave him a natural reason for bringing up the rear. In all that long and silent ride, Chip held his gaze upon the dim moving figure of Blink Roberts and wondered what was in the man's mind. Whatever it was, it certainly failed to include a suspicion of the knowledge hidden behind the stern face of the quiet young fellow behind him.

And so they jogged along the rutted trail, three silent riders and a pack horse and a flaxen-maned yearling colt, looking at peace with their world and with themselves, in no great hurry to get where they were going.

XX

A FINE SCHEME COOKED UP

A DEPRESSED FEELING OF UTTER FAILURE CAUGHT CHIP unawares as they rode up the creek into Flying U Coulee, lying so quiet under the stars, with the young moon just sliding backwards over the western line of hills. What he had decided was the wisest plan he could devise suddenly became no plan at all, or at the best a cheap gallery play. The truth was, he had stared too long at Blink Roberts' back. He began to wonder what he was going to do with him when they reached the ranch and he wished to thunder he had left him back at the Hobble-O where he belonged.

Back there it had seemed the only sensible course to take. Old Shep and J.G. had to get together right away—no two ways about that—and Chip had been afraid to leave Blink on the ranch. No telling what he was supposed to do or what might happen. For all he knew, it might be Blink's job to burn Shep out. And there were five other strange men for Snuffle to keep an eye on. . . . No, the safest way was to bring Blink along, he guessed.

But what was he going to do with him now? He wished he had told Shep more about it. But there again he had felt he would be taking too long a chance of the thing leaking out. Shep would maybe have wanted to handle the thing alone. . . . No, the best way was to bring Shep and Blink over to the Flying U. Thank the Lord, he knew this bunch to a fare-you-well. If he could handle the first few minutes all right, without tipping his hand too much to Blink, or letting Blink pull anything, he'd be all right.

Just the same, he hated the role he had given himself. If they gave him the laugh—if they didn't take what he told them and let it go as it lay . . . It did sound pretty darned far-fetched—as if he'd had a pipe dream of some kind.

They were at the corrals now. In spite of his worry, it was like coming home. There was Weary's top horse, a buckskin called Fiddler, calmly munching hay in the corner he always appropriated for himself, even at the cost of much squealing and biting. There were the other horses he knew—a night horse apiece for the Happy Family, as if they were prepared to mount and ride at a moment's notice. Milt Cummings was the cause of that, he knew. The significance of that string of top horses in the corral at night heartened him, gave him the assurance his weary nerves needed. His tired shoulders straightened as his chin went up. Come hell or high water, the Flying U was a solid wall at his back. You bet your sweet life.

"I'll leave my horse outside," said Blink—the first words he had spoken on the trip. "He'd raise hell with all them strange cayuses in there."

Shep grunted some unintelligible reply to that. Chip was inside, pulling the saddle off Mike. Some of the other boys would drag the pack off Jeff, he was thinking. Now that he was home again, he felt as though every problem he had could be left to the other boys. His job was almost done. He had to tell them what he knew—after that, he could roll in his blankets and sleep the clock around.

It was, in fact, the first really relaxed moment he had had since that windy day more than a month ago, when he and Weary had first discovered the butchered beef. Walking up the path to the bunkhouse his stride lengthened perceptibly. It wasn't so late yet, he was thinking. Couldn't be much after ten o'clock. And though the lights were out, maybe the boys weren't asleep yet. Or if they were, it didn't matter much.

The other two walking single file behind him, Chip went into blackness only a little lightened by the starry squares of windows. From a well-known corner, Weary sat up staring at Chip's face lighted by the lamp, as he set the chimney within its brass guards.

"Mamma! Where'd you drop down from, Chip?"

Heads bobbed up, profane exclamations of surprise filled the long low room; vituperations hurled at Chip in tones of affectionate welcome made him grin while he swore back at them.

Then he sobered. "Get up, you wall-eyed yahoos. I'll go get J.G. over here. . . ."

"What's broke loose now, Chip?" . . . "What's eatin' on yuh?"

To these and other questions Chip made no reply. Again he was feeling slightly foolish, as if maybe he should have done this differently. Calling a mass meeting like this before he'd open up with what he knew—he was going to feel like seven kinds of a fool when he got ready to speak his piece, if they didn't believe him. They'd maybe think he was crazy. Sometimes he kind of thought so himself.

But he went doggedly on with his job. He'd tell them—they could do as they pleased about believing him. Damn it, he wasn't responsible for the way it was going to sound. . . .

J.G. gave him a strange intent stare from his bed, then without a word he reached for his pants. "Milt on the rampage again?" And when Chip shook his head, J.G. grunted something under his breath and followed to the bunk house, buckling on his gun as he went. Not that he would need it, but because habit goes on with the routine of dressing when a man's thoughts are elsewhere.

The Happy Family, half dressed and looking owlishly uneasy and curious, sat on the edge of their rumpled beds and rolled cigarettes while they waited. By the rough board table old Shep sat crowding tobacco into his pipe, his face a lined mask above the whiskers. And by the door Blink Roberts moved aside when Chip and Jim Whitmore came in.

"I was following some tracks this morning, down in that canyon where I picked up those horses last summer," Chip began, without prelude or apology. "Struck the trail Milt's gang had made with those cowhide boots, getting over this way from the Lazy Ladder and back again. Or I thought I had. I followed it through an ungodly mess of dry washes and little gulches and deep gorges, to where it forked, and I took the right-hand fork. My horse heard something ahead, so I left him and climbed up the side of that crack in the hill I was following, and I came out where I could look down on Big Butch's corral and the front part of his stable."

"Thought you said it was the Lazy Ladder," Cal Emmett blurted.

"I thought so myself till I got where I could see. Butch was down there by the stable, talking to some fellows that had just ridden in, evidently. They hunkered down and proceeded to mill over their affairs—" His glance moved from old Shep to J.G. "I thought you folks better hear about it right away."

With fingers that shook a little, he started to roll a cigarette, gave it up and held tobacco sack and papers clenched in his hand. The flesh on his thin face seemed to harden and shrink, like the face of an old man. His voice, too, was harsh and had a husky note when he spoke.

"They've got a fine little scheme cooked up; Butch and the Lazy Ladder and most of—well, all of the Cow Island bunch, as near as I could tell—"

"Figurin' they'll raid this outfit, ay?" J.G. anticipated shrewdly. "I been wonderin'—"

"Raid hell! They've got their sights raised to killing

you off, wiping out the Flying U and the Hobble-O and all the nesters scattered up and down the creeks—make a clean sweep, that's all!" Chip's voice cracked on the last words. "They're going whole hog. Then some of their outlaw friends from down Wyoming way will trail in cattle and horses and annex all the range. They're figuring on having what Butch calls an outlaw paradise. They've got men lined up in Dry Lake—up there somewhere, anyway—to protect them on the north, and with Cow Island keeping tally on the river, they'll be riding high, wide and handsome from the Bear Paws to the Missouri."

"The dirty sons—uh guns!" swore Shorty, only that is not just what he said. "And what do they figure we'll be doin' all this time?"

"Occupying your six feet of earth," Chip told him succinctly. "All that beef stealing was to pull the Flying U into a scrap with the Hobble-O. Milt did his damndest to cook that up. Then they'd jump in and do a little shooting in the back. They didn't give a cuss whether Shep and Snuffle got hung or not. If they could have got J.G. and Shep locking horns, and all this outfit killed off in the fight, word would go out that the two outfits had fought to a finish. And they'd make sure that J.G. was one of the casualties. . . ." He flung out a hand in the expressive gesture he used to invite one's imagination to finish a picture for him.

"Well," slow-witted Slim stated heavily, "it didn't work, by golly!"

"It didn't the other night, simply because Milt took the bit in his teeth and thought he'd open the ball with a lynching bee. The weather turned off warm and he figured the Hobble-O was through hauling out beef—and then he was sore too, because you fellows wouldn't set into the game with him. Butch cussed him out plenty for being too previous." Chip bit his underlip, trying to steady it.

"What for scheme they got now?" J.G. wanted to know. "You happen to hear?"

"Enough to fill in the gaps. A lot of gun fighters came up from the south and they're at Butch's place. A lot more have been drifting in to Cow Island. I gathered there's about twenty or more, all told. Then the Lazy Ladder has been hiring a round-up crew too, the last couple of days." He slanted a meaning look at old Shep. "Tomorrow night there's going to be a big setting at Butch's. They're going to lay their plans then as to just how the play is to be made. But I got it straight enough that J.G. is to get his ticket about the first thing. Dry-gulch him, I guess. That would leave the Flying U without a boss—nobody owning the stock or having any authority to go ahead.

"Butch told the fellows—strangers, they were—all about the Flying U, and how it's the key ranch of this country, north of the river. He said J.G. didn't have any relatives and he said"—Chip stopped to swallow—"he said when Jim Whitmore was found with a bullet in him, that would be the time to clean up on the nesters. And while that was taking place, all you fellows would be taken care of—leaving the nesters, I suppose, for the last, and stringing them up for a bunch of wholesale killings they didn't do. He said it would be a cinch to put the blame where it would do the most good."

"That's quite a contract," some one remarked, in a grim tone.

"And surprise is the essence of their contract," Chip said, with a bleak kind of humor. "I don't know just how they mean to go about starting, now that Milt has tipped his hand. Butch was plenty sore about that. It would have been all right," he added laconically, "if it had worked the way Milt expected. They'd have put the blame on the Flying U and then the Vigilantes would have cleaned up this outfit, and half the job would have been done. That's the way Butch wanted to work it, but he wanted to wait till this new gang pulled in. Now—"

"Now," old Shep snarled interruption, "they got the Hobble-O to reckon with. I've got seven fightin' men at my back. They better not overlook that fact!"

"Butch said leave it to Blink Roberts—" Chip could have bitten his tongue in two for the blunder, but the words were out. He glanced swiftly at Blink, gave a sharp cry of warning and reached for his gun.

"You damn fool, this is how it starts!" Blink shouted, and fired from his hip as he jerked the door open. While their eardrums still rang with the roar of his forty-five, he slammed the door behind him and ran.

Some one was on the floor and Chip jumped over him and caught the door while it still quivered from Blink's hurried exit. His bullet sped after the fleeing spy, caught up with him and whirled him half around, breaking his stride. But he did not go down. He ran on, shouting back curses, emptying his six-shooter at the lighted doorway.

XXI

ONE SPY THE LESS

THE HAPPY FAMILY RUSHED LIKE STAMPEDING broncos through the bunkhouse door and gave chase. Ahead of them ran Chip, shooting at the fleeing shadow and calling back to the others as he went.

"Get him—don't let him get away— It's all my own damn fault—" He stumbled, tried to catch himself and pitched forward as the others tore past.

A wave of nausea that was partly mental seized him when he attempted to regain his feet and go on. He wasn't hit, or if he was, he couldn't tell where. It was a sage root or something of the sort that had caught his toe and tripped him. His ankle hurt with a sickening pain—but more than that, despair had him by the throat. That he could have forgotten Blink Roberts and the part he was to play seemed incredible. Yet it had happened. His mind had held nothing but the horror that was being hatched. He had given Blink the cue to shoot some one and go warn Butch and Milt.

Like hounds on hot scent, the boys were giving tongue down there by the corral. An orange flower blossomed by the stable as a gunshot smashed through the darkness. Another and another. Then silence, followed by murmurous sounds. A match blaze flared, went out. A second glow cupped between palms bent low, lighting something on the ground. Horses in the corral were snorting and there was a trampling of feet as they surged across to the farther fence.

In the doorway behind Chip the querulous voice of J.G. called out impatiently, "Git back here, some of you fellers! I want some help here! Don't take more'n a regiment to ketch one man— Shorty! Somebuddy go git some hot water! Daw-gone it—"

Steadying himself against the wall, Chip moved toward him giddily, his knees still unaccountably wabbling under him. He remembered now, some one on the floor had almost tripped him. "Is—any one hurt?"

J.G. craned forward, peering through the gloom. "That you? Yuh hit?" He reached out a hand, got Chip by the shoulder as he swayed. "Git in here! My Lord, if some of them crazy loons don't show up— What's the matter?" His blue eyes looked black and piercing as he stared into his youngest cowboy's face. "You're white around the gills as a dyin' fish."

"I—I don't know . . . I'm—just—sick. I—"

"About time you caved in. Daw-gone chump—don't know when to quit . . . What you think you are—a gove'ment mule or somethin'? There. You lay down there an' behave yourself." He gently propelled Chip limping to the nearest bunk and pushed him down upon it. "If there ain't men enough in this outfit to take a holt now and handle this job, daw-gone it, I'll go hire me some real hands."

Chip only half heard him. In a vague and dreamy

fashion he knew that he was on Shorty's bunk, and alongside it there seemed to lie a vast gulf of velvety blackness into which he wanted to slide so that he could sleep. Never in his life had he wanted anything so much as to let go all holds and sleep forever.

But he couldn't do that. A nagging guilt and a responsibility held him to the bunk. He mustn't slip over the edge into the blackness. He had let Blink Roberts shoot some one and get away—down to tell Butch and Milt the Flying U outfit was wise to their hellish scheme. He had a terribly clear picture of Blink down there at the Big Butch cabin, spilling the news. He had to go after Blink and bring him back—in a minute, when he had rested a little.

It was his fault that Blink got away. Killed J.G.—or no, he guessed it wasn't J.G. either, because he heard him swearing. Swearing at him, because he had made a damned mess of things. What ever got into him, to tell everything before Blink? He guessed he thought the boys would grab Blink—or—if he weren't so damned sleepy, he'd know why he forgot that Blink was standing there by the door, wearing two guns—Blink wasn't such a hell of a bad man or he'd have slaughtered the whole works. . . .

In a minute he'd have to go bring him back. It was up to him—he was the one who played right into Blink's hands. But that bunk—there was something the matter with it. He kept slipping over the edge. . . . Polly made it that way just for devilment. It was hard to hang onto—or maybe he didn't have much of a grip on himself. Seems like he hadn't slept or rested for a month—and his damned arm aching like the toothache . . .

Some one was talking—saying they got him. Got who? If he could just get a grip on something, so he could lift himself up where he could find out—find out . . . Big Butch was a Judas—treating him like a long-lost brother, and all the time planning to massacre—kill off all the honest men. . . . Make an outlaw paradise, hunh? . . . He'd show Butch—tell him he had another think coming . . . In a minute, he would—just as soon as he could . . . He was down so far now . . . so far he couldn't even hear who it was they had got. Butch, maybe—the Judas . . .

So Chip's rambling thoughts—if such they could be called—drifted off into oblivion, and he slipped over the edge into a deep, dreamless sleep of exhaustion.

Six feet away from him J.G. and Shorty bent together over another bunk where Shep lay with his lips pulled so tightly together his whiskers stood straight out. His eyes were squinted half-shut, staring up into the faces of the two and trying to read their minds. Shorty held a pan of pinkish water smelling strongly of carbolic acid, into which J.G. dipped a torn corner of clean flour sack.

Shep's side was bared, surprisingly white and smooth save where the ugly torn hole in front showed ragged lips from which the blood seeped persistently. At the back, through several inches of stringy muscle and tissue, a round little hole, bluish around the rim, received scant attention.

"You hadn't oughta pushed in between us like that,"

Jim Whitmore grumbled, his voice gruff to hide his emotion. “Little more, and all hell couldn’t ’a’ saved yuh. One rib’s busted, but I guess your innards was outa the way. Prob’ly glued together like a starved chicken, and they don’t take up no room scarcely—you’re so daw-gone skinny.”

“How’s m’ liver?” Shep’s voice was weak, anxious.

J.G. squinted and considered. “Wel-l, if she lays where she’d oughta, she was outa line with the bullet. Don’t seem to be nothin’ punctured bad but straight meat. That rib’ll have to knit before you can git around much.”

“Just when I’m goin’ to be needed!”

“Chip,” said Shorty heavily, “had oughta told us about that feller. Didn’t you know, Shep?”

Shep shook his head. “Only what the kid hinted. Said I’d have to fetch Blink along with us. He never said why.”

“Damn poor management, looks like to me,” Shorty criticized. “Left him standin’ right there, where he had the drop on the hull bunch of us. Biggest wonder in the world he didn’t make a killin’ in here.”

Weary came in, looked down at Shep for a minute, and turned to where Chip lay slack, one leg drooping over the bunk’s edge. He glanced across at Shorty. “You’re a mile off, Shorty. A bigger wonder is that this sick kid here got down in to Butch’s place and got out again with all the dope on their plans, and then got up here with it and brought Blink along. Hell, he ain’t endowed with omniscience, is he?” And when Shorty’s face went blank, he clarified the statement:

"You couldn't expect Chip to think of everything and read a man's mind at the same time, could you?"

Shorty grunted. "All I'm thinkin' is, that dirty hound come within an ace of killin' J.G. He would of, if Shep hadn't pushed in between."

"Chip done all right," J.G. told them gruffly. "My fault as much as anybody's. He told me on the way in here what-fer coyote he'd brought along. I was so worked up over the hull cussed scheme I forgot to keep an eye on Blink. Daw-gone it, Shorty, don't go blamin' Chip any."

"Hell, I ain't blamin' him," Shorty recanted. "I was just sayin' it's a damn close call for more'n Shep, here. Might of cost us dear."

Others were coming in anxious over Shep and trying to appear casual and unalarmed. "Well, we got 'im, by golly," Slim stated heavily, looking around as if it were news to all save himself. "Big Butch sure will wait a long time for any spyin' from that there jasper. Say, who's got his guns an' belt?"

By the bunk, drawing off Chip's boots as if he were disrobing a dead man, Chip lay so inert, Weary looked up and tilted his head toward the table by the window. "Over there. He sure was heeled for bear, all right." He looked at Dick Bird, huge and helpless in his diffidence, standing near by. "Catch hold of him, will you, Dickybird? Raise him up so I can get his coat off without maulin' that game arm."

As if he were handling a child, Dickybird lifted Chip's head and shoulders in his arms. "Didn't git hit again, did he?"

Weary shook his head. "Just all in, I guess. Fine large day he's had. Maybe we better take a look at that arm while we're about it. What yuh think?"

"I've got some salve that's awful good," Penny volunteered. "Swab some of that on, why don't yuh? Helps the itchin' when a bullet hole starts to git well."

"Dig her up, then. Won't do any hurt to slap some on."

J.G. turned around from Shep's bedside, pulling down his sleeves. "Ted and Penny, you go round up a team and hitch 'em to the bed-wagon," he said, in the tone of a round-up boss. "Pile in lots of hay and blankets—we better haul Shep home b'fore daylight. I want the rest of you fellers to saddle up and go pass the word around amongst the nesters. Them that's got families, tell 'em to bring their folks here. With camp outfit, so they can be comf'table." He looked at Shep for confirmation and received a nod of approval.

"My place is too—close to trouble," Shep explained. "Better have 'em here."

"Get Johnson, Pilgreen—all them fellers that's moved in on the creeks, and up in the draws this side uh the Bear Paws. Tell 'em what's bein' cooked up for 'em down in the Badlands and git 'em here, quick as the Lord'll let 'em come. Tell 'em it's their funeral as much as ours, and we need all the men we can git."

"If you can make out alone here, J.G., I'll go along," Shorty was reaching for his rifle.

"Sure, go along. Daw-gone it, it'll take every man on the ranch to git the word around before mornin' and not miss anybody. And say! Make it plain that we don't want no inklin' to git outside. You remember what Chip said about their havin' men scattered around up this way—Dry Lake and so on. That's how Shep happened to git let in, hirin' one of their men unbeknown to him."

Shep lifted a hand. "They're liable to miss Blink tomorrow, if they're watchin' my place," he pointed out. "They might be expectin' him to meet 'em somewhere—with what he'd picked up."

"All he picked up is about four hunks of lead, by golly," Slim gloated.

"They'll think it's funny if he don't show."

"They'll think some other things is a damn sight funnier," J.G. snorted. "Well, you toll off the riders, Shorty. Make a circle—two by two. Might be all right to ride alone, but we ain't takin' no chances we don't have to."

"Chip took a chance and rode alone," Weary commented, with a side glance at Shorty.

"Hell, I wasn't diggin' my spurs into Chip in p'ticular," Shorty answered the look. "No need givin' me the bad eye—I know he's a go-getter all right and that they don't come any gamer than that kid. Just the same, if that feller Blink had been onto his job, this woulda looked like a slaughterhouse in here. It sure was takin' an awful chance, what I mean. I don't back down from that."

Since he was their boss under Jim Whitmore himself, no one took up the argument. Even Weary, jealous for Chip's honor though he was, knew that Shorty spoke the truth and said no more about it. It was an incredible blunder and one that no normal man would ever have made.

"He was dead on his feet when he got here," J.G. summed it up in his querulous voice. "Daw-gone it, I don't want to hear no more about it." His tone changed as the Happy Family crowded toward the door. "That feller way up next the mountain—git him too. Tell 'em all to fog over here quick as they can make it—like the Injuns had broke loose off the rese'-vation er something. We got to move fast—make that plain to 'em."

"Darn right," Shorty nodded from the doorway. "You goin' down with Shep?"

"No," said J.G., "I'll be here. Ted and Penny'll be enough to git him home, all right. There won't be anything break loose till after tomorra night, prob'ly."

"Well, all right. We'll have the nesters rounded up by daylight or we'll know the reason why." And Shorty closed the door behind him—softly, in deference to the sleeping boy and the old man who had taken the bullet meant for another.

XXII

MAKE READY FOR WAR

WHILE THE BIG DIPPER WHEELED ITS SLOW MAJESTIC march round the North Star, Chip lay drugged in the bottomless pool of sleep. And while he slept, the message he had brought out of the Badlands took life and form in the brains and bodies of men and drove them forth upon grim business through the night.

While he lay as moveless as the dead, the cluck of wagon came up from the corrals and ceased for a space outside the bunkhouse door. Ted Culver's voice, subdued but holding harsh authority in its tones, admonished the restless sleek team that did not want to stand still but backed and sidled, cramping the front wheel against the wagon box. "Stand still, you wall-eyed, hammer-headed thus-and-so's!"

Walking carefully to and fro, into the cabin and out to the wagon standing there, blurred in the chill starlight, blankets were spread upon crisp fragrant hay of last summer. An impish gusty breeze caught a blanket corner from Penny's hand, snapped it like the pop of a whip. The uneasy horses jumped ahead and both men swore, Penny clawing for the high spring seat to steady himself, Ted Culver leaning backward, feet wide apart on the ground, sawing with the lines.

"Make that damned team stand still, can't yuh?" hurrying Penny snarled, angry because he had come near falling.

"Not while you go poppin' blankets behind 'em," Ted snarled back, adding profane phrases born of worry.

Penny replied in kind and finished his careful bed-making. As he climbed down, he spoke from a wider experience than Ted's. "Say, you better unhook them broncs till we git him in and bedded down. Liable to raise hell with him, if the horses git to cuttin' up just when we're loadin' him in."

"Why didn't yuh think of it before the damn buzzard-heads pulled both arms off?" Ted grumbled and acted upon the suggestion, Penny helping.

They loaded Shep in, lifting him carefully in a blanket, J.G. in the wagon, steadying the disposal of his shrunken, pain-racked body upon the springy hay. "Better rustle a coupla fur coats to spread over him. It's goin' to be cold as all gitout, ridin' back here. He ain't got the circulation—"

"I'm hot as hell-fire right now!"

"Might feel that way now, but you could ketch cold in that side just the same."

He spread two heavy coats, tucked in the blankets, pushed up the hay beneath Shep's head into a snug hollowed nest. Penny and Ted were hitching up the team again.

With the night breeze roughing his graying hair around the bald spot, J.G. climbed down and went to where Penny was hooking the tugs of the nigh horse.

"You got plenty of ca'tridges, Penny? 'Tain't anyways likely 't you'll be molested, but you want to be ready. If you have any trouble at all, it'll be after you hit the Hobble-O coulee."

"I'll sure keep both eyes peeled, J.G."

And around on Ted's side— "Drive careful, Ted. And you boys git right back here. Better tell Snuffle and the bunch what's up—Shep's liable to be out of his head when yuh git there. Tell Snuffle to stick close to the coulee tomorrow and wait till I give 'em orders."

"How is he, J.G.?" Ted's lowered voice inquired.

"Perty bad off, to my way of thinkin'. Bad place to git shot. Mis' Taylor's good as a doctor, though. Well, you better git goin'. Careful how you hit the bumps, now!"

He climbed up a wheel, peered down at the wounded man. "How yuh comin', Shep? Lay'n all right and comf'table?"

"I'm—all right. Long as they git me home—"

"They'll git yuh home, all right. Well, so long—see yuh later, Shep."

Long after the wagon and the two cowboys side by side on the high spring seat had merged with the night shadows down by the corral, J.G. stood abstractedly gazing down the way they had gone. When the rattle of the wagon down the creek trail was stilled by distance, and the silence seeped in again and filled the coulee to the rim, and only the darkness and the brilliant pattern of stars remained, he turned and went inside, groping abstractedly for his pipe in his pocket.

Already on the high benchland, over bald ridges, down into coulees and creek bottoms the boys of the Flying U were galloping, two fleet riders here, two more speeding in another direction, another couple riding north to the foothills of the Bear Paws—wherever the venturesome small ranchers had nested their cabins in a sheltered spot where there was water fit to drink and where a little wild hay could be cut and stacked to feed a saddle horse, a team—perhaps a milk cow or two. In the last year or two, a dozen or so had moved in within riding distance of the Flying U. And these must be warned of the monstrous outrage being plotted.

Some had wives, two or three were feeding young mouths precariously, while they got a foothold on the range. Several were bachelors living like hermits in some secluded coulee. Most of them were honest fellows; but if they now and then ate "slow elk" it was only when necessity drove them to poach upon their neighbors, and Jim Whitmore made no quarrel over what he could only suspect.

It was the women who furnished the surprises that night.

"Who'll do the milkin' and take care of the chickens, if I go traipsin' off over to the Flyin' U? My land, it ain't like an Injun massacree, is it?"

"No, ma'am, I guess it ain't that bad. But Jim Whitmore kinda thought you'd be scared to stay alone for a couple days maybe—"

"Scared, my foot! If I was scared to stay alone, I wouldn't be here in the first place. Don't I stay alone all durin' round-up time and when my man is off puttin' up hay?"

"J.G. thought maybe it'd be safer at the Flyin' U till we get this thing settled."

"Well, my conscience! Ain't you fellows goin' to keep that miserable gang of cutthroats busy fightin'?"

"Yes, ma'am." This was Weary. "We sure hope to."

"Well, then, seems to me the safest place for me is right to home, where I belong. They ain't goin' to have time to come larrupin' away off over here. And if they do—well, get Big Butch in front of the old shotgun and I couldn't tell him from a chicken hawk. You go on and clean 'em up. You don't have to worry a mite about me."

At every cabin it was the same. Called from their beds and their sleep, the nesters listened and turned to pick up rifles, buckle on their cartridge belts, and their spurs. But the women's thoughts flew to the cow, the chickens, the pigs. Perhaps an early calf in the sod-roofed stable tipped the scale. They would not leave, but hurried their men off into the night, fierce-eyed because of what threatened their lives and their homes.

Goin' to be strung up for killin' Jim Whitmore, huh? Have the word go out that the Bear Paw nesters were starting a range war against the Flying U! Why, thunder! How would any of them ever get through the winter, if the Flying U didn't give 'em work through the summer? What the devil would they want to start fightin' against their own bread and butter for? They saddled and rode, rifles across their thighs. Cowboys, most of them; range-hardened men, every one.

Patsy's pet Plymouth Rock rooster, bestirring himself on his roost promptly at two o'clock in the morning, stood up in the dark of the henhouse, shook the fine ruff on his neck and sent his sonorous call out into the night. "Oo-oo-*oo-o*-oo-*OOO-OOo!*"

The first of the nesters were just riding down over the coulee rim on the north. "Gettin' along toward mornin'," said one. "Rooster's crowin'—we made good time."

"Wonder if they figure on startin' the ball rollin' today?"

"Search me. The sooner the quicker, far as I'm concerned."

"Yeah. Same here. They got their gall, all right. But d' yuh know, Jim, if nobody'd got wise to their play, they coulda made it stick, all right."

"You're damn tootin' they could. Wonder how the Flyin' U got next to it!"

"Search me. There wasn't no time to find out. They just rode up an' give me the word and pulled out."

"Same here. They wanted me to hitch up and bring the old woman over here to stay. But, hell, you couldn't git her off the ranch with dynamite."

"They'll never git this far up, anyway. Not with old J.G. on his hind legs, waitin' for 'em."

Below them the coulee lay steeped in silence threaded by the bell-clear crowing of the old speckled rooster. Over their heads as they rode, the Big Dipper stood tiptilted. Job's Coffin twinkled diamond bright.

"Wonder how many Big Butch has got?"

"Shorty never said. Imported some from Hole-in-the-Wall, chances is. That's where Butch come from, they tell me."

Down in the corral a horse whinnied. A door—J.G.'s—opened; light streamed out.

"Damn fools, they'd oughta blow out the light before they open that door."

From down the creek a man whistled a shrill, rather complicated run of notes.

"That's Weary Davidson. I know that whistle," the one called Jim remarked, as he touched a spur to his horse. "All serene so far, by the looks. I guess the gang is still powwowin' down at Butch's."

"We'll give 'em something to powwow about!"

"You bet your sweet life!" And when Weary's call was repeated, he answered it with a cowboy yell, the *Yip-yip-yoee* of the Flying U. Up on the bench behind him faint echo sounded. Behind that still another shrill yell. Like wolves when the hunting call goes ululating out under the moon, from far and near wraithlike ribbons of sound came drifting into the coulee. A yip-yip, the thud of galloping hoofs, the far-off chuckle of the wagon returning.

It was a reckless thing to do. They had expected to ride in stealthily. The man who cursed because J.G. stood in the doorway with light behind him gave a throaty whoop as he charged down through the willows and across an elbow of the creek. Reckless, and yet it was not without some measure of assurance. That first whistle, coming from a rider who had taken the trails nearest Big Butch's hide-out, had released a tension. Without a word it had spread the news that the trails to the south were yet clear. The rattling wagon confirmed it. For this night, the northern range was safe.

In the cook house a big hanging lamp blossomed. Sparks from dry, burning sage bark floated briefly above the roof. Riders converged upon the saddle-horse corral, calling rough greetings as they rode up and dismounted. Penny and Ted drove into the yard, jumped down over the wheel and started to unhitch.

"Well, how yuh make it?"

"Fine and dandy. Never had a word uh trouble."

“Shep stand the trip all right?”

“Seemed to. Face looked all ganted up when we packed him into the house, but he never made any holler or fuss.”

Later, to J.G., Penny reported, “Nary a whimper of anything around the Hobble-O. Empty as a line camp on Fourth of July. If anybody’s night-herdin’ Shep’s place, they sure as hell never let on they saw or heard a thing.”

“You tell Snuffle what I said?”

“We sure did. He said he’d keep the bunch busy shoein’ horses and gettin’ things shaped up for spring round-up, till he heard from you. He was certainly surprised about Blink Roberts, but he thinks the rest is all right. Just the same, he ain’t goin’ to spill any news of what’s bein’ cooked up. Snuffle thinks the safest bet is to watch ’em close and tell ’em nothin’.”

“Yeah, Snuffle Jones is a good man down there,” J.G. assented. “Well, roll in and git yourselves some sleep.”

That was the order he gave to cowboys and nesters alike, as they arrived. A shrewd man, Jim Whitmore. Because he could not tell what another day might reveal, he caught at this respite and used it to freshen his men and horses. Well he knew that eyes heavy with sleep lose something of their keenness, and that tired hands are less steady; nerves must be steel when these men faced Big Butch.

Stars paled and the sun rose and looked upon a sleeping ranch. But hidden amongst the boulders, on the rim that walled the coulee, two men kept watch against a surprise attack, even though it seemed from Chip's terse report that Big Butch did not plan to strike so soon. One never knew; and so it would not do to take a chance.

By sunrise every man north of the Hobble-O and south of the Bear Paws had arrived; fourteen nesters and two grizzled trappers malodorously proclaiming their calling and looking competent to whip a dozen of anything from Big Butch's gang to grizzlies. Twenty-three noses around the breakfast table wrinkled at the rancid smell of half-cured pelts coming from these two, though the owners of the noses were careful to make no comment. Trappers are touchy fellows, and these two had fought Indians in their day and were going to be extremely valuable.

"Well," J.G. observed, as he straddled a bench and sat down to his breakfast, "I guess everybody's accounted for. Fill up—no tellin' when we'll git another chance."

"Yuh goin' to start action right off?" someone down at the other end of the table wanted to know.

Ears pricked up to hear the answer to that, but J.G. took his time, spearing two pancakes onto his plate and helping himself to meat and potatoes before he spoke.

"The boy that knows the lay of the land ain't woke up yet, and I want he should get his rest. When he gits up and I've had another talk with 'im, I'll know better what the plans are. Just stick around and take it easy—but be ready to jump off the bed-ground at a minute's notice. Pass the molasses, somebody."

XXIII
CHIP RIDES AGAIN

WITH HIS PIPE COOLING IN HIS PALM, JIM WHITMORE stared out through his cabin doorway, where the sun shone in straight to prove the hour was midday. “There’s times,” he said, “when bein’ law-abidin’ ties a man’s hands and gives crooks all the advantage.”

“Meaning this is one of the times?” Sitting on a corner of J.G.’s table, with his hat pushed back from his lean sensitive face, Chip turned a somber questioning gaze upon his boss.

“It sure is. If we was their stripe, we could go after ’em right now, on the strength of what you heard. But seein’ we ain’t none of us outlaws, we can’t just ride down there and string ’em up ’cause they shot off their mouths about what they was aimin’ to do. C’rell talk’s most generally wind. Ain’t there some way of ketchin’ ’em in some skulduggery er other?”

“Well, you might wait till somebody bushwhacks you,” Chip told him dryly. “From the way Butch talked, I don’t believe you’d have to wait long.”

Haze thickened between them, J.G. smoked so furiously, “Daw-gone it, you come bustin’ into camp with a story that’d stampede a graveyard—”

“Have you got any doubt of its being true?”

“Hell, who’s talkin’ about doubts? ’Course it’s true! But that ain’t sayin’ I know which way to turn. What we’d oughta do,” he went on more calmly, “is go down there and clean out the gang and do it quick. But there's the daw-gone law. Fu'thermore, there's such a thing as justice. Yuh can't go by talk an' guesswork. So fur, Big Butch ain't never made a crooked move toward us, ner the Hobble-O either."

"No, he's merely been laying his plans to wipe out both outfits and glom all this range for him and his outlaw friends. He wouldn't bother with one killing, or even two. What he figures on is killing on a big scale—and have it look as if he was pushed into it, trying to uphold the law!" Bitter sarcasm was in Chip's look and tone. He finished with a snort of disgust.

"Hear him say just where they aim to make a start?"

"No. There was something said about the Hobble-O, but nothing definite. That's to be settled tonight, when all of them—those new imported outlaws—get in."

"Any idea how many they figure on?"

"No, I haven't. I could find out, though, easily enough."

"Huh?" J.G.'s head jerked around as though something had stung him. "Find out how?"

Chip drew in his underlip, raked even teeth across it. His eyes had suddenly sharpened to an intent frowning stare. "I could high-tail it down there again and get in where I could see—and hear."

"You could git your fool brains blowed out," J.G. snorted. "If you're that sick of livin', I can have somebuddy knock yuh in the head with an ax."

"I wouldn't be taking any great chance. I know their secret trail in from the big canyon, where their outlaw trail heads through to the east. They won't be using that trail tonight—it was mostly for getting over onto Flying U range, I think. After dark, I can get right up to the cabin."

"You can stay outa there too!"

"It'd be pickings. The cabin sets back in a thicket of brush and trees, and there's a little window set pretty high—about up to my shoulder. Some ambitious yahoo threw a boot or fired a shot or some darned thing—anyway, there's a hole about the size of a hen's egg in the glass." His lips twitched into a half smile. "I sure would like to pin my ears back outside that window when their big powwow comes off tonight."

J.G. moved restlessly on the box that served him for a seat. "You'd play hell, eavesdroppin' on that gang!"

"It's a cinch." Chip's tenseness eased a shade. With a purely automatic impulse, his hand moved to the pocket where he kept the makings. "I had that all figured out last night," he said, and blew a gentle breath into his book of papers, singling out a leaf. "I can hear all that's said in that cabin and I can count noses and bring you the tally." He began tearing a neat, thin strip from the paper. "You can—"

"I can hog-tie yuh till you come to your senses, dawgone yuh!" But by his tone and his look, J.G. betrayed how the idea tempted him. "Anyway, it wouldn't work. Time you got back up here they—"

"Not here," Chip cut him short. "You could take this bunch to the Hobble-O and wait there. That's the place to work from, anyway. You must have come by a shortcut down over the rim the other night—why not have some of the boys cut over that way again? They can find out if anybody's cached up there, watching the coulee, and drag 'em down off their perch."

"Yeah—and then what?" By his tone J.G. was merely holding back his veto until the plan was all before him.

"Well, it's none of my business—you're running this—but if I was doing it, I'd send a few men down there right now, J.G. Nobody's going to get excited if they see a bunch of the boys ride in to the Hobble-O this afternoon; not if there aren't too many and if they ride along like nothing much is on their minds. You, for instance, and two or three more."

"Me, huh?"

"Yes, you. Nobody's going to take a potshot at you down there—not when they're planning to lay the blame on these nesters up this way, when you do meet up with the hot end of a bullet. That'll put you down there where you can take charge of things and keep cases on what Butch's gang is up to." He paused to lick his cigarette into shape. "Then the rest could slip in there after dark." He set the cigarette between his lips and hunted a match in his pocket. "All you'd need to do then is lie low till I get the goods on the bunch and pass it on to you."

"They'd pass on your soul to hell," J.G. made gloomy prediction. "Chip, you know daw-gone well you wouldn't have a Chinaman's chance, down in there. Sounds all right and you're just crazy enough to tackle it if I'd let yuh—but I won't. It's too damn risky."

"Risky?" Chip gave a short laugh, as he fanned the

match blaze out. “Hell, I’ve been taking a heap bigger risk than that, everyday since I started digging into that beef rustling. It was a risk when I rode into Butch’s place and boned him about stealing beef, but I got away with it all right.”

“Butch was just stallin’ you along. He wasn’t ready to open up and show his hand. It’s different now.”

“This is going to be a cinch, I tell you. Why, look! I spent a full week down there. I know that layout as well as I do this coulee. I know right where Butch will put a couple of men in the pass—I bet I could show you the rocks they’ll hide in while they’re on guard. And if he’s got any suspicions of what the Hobble-O may do, he’ll put a guard farther down in the canyon. But—”

“It don’t make a daw-gone bit of difference how many guards he puts in the canyon—”

“Maybe not, only that canyon is supposed to be the only way into Butch’s place. That way I found is their secret trail—so damned secret they always put boots on their horses when they go in or out that way. Unless you knew, you never would find it. I did, because I saw the kind of marks Mike made, and picked out others like them.”

“They’ll pick you out, if you don’t keep clear.”

“I beg to differ with you there,” Chip replied, with that persistence which made him what he was. “They don’t use that trail very often, I imagine. It seems to be a short cut out east and they duck through that way to get onto your range for their rustlings. No reason why any of them should come out that way today or tonight—it's the canyon they'll be using and the trail over to the Lazy Ladder. They won't put a guard out back, because they don't know anybody is wise to it. It won't enter their heads that anyone will come in that way."

J.G. shifted his position again. "Well, if you got the hang of readin' their minds," he grumbled, "they's no use goin'. You can set here and make a guess at what they're cookin' up."

Chip grinned in spite of himself. "I may seem to think I'm a hell of a feller," he drawled, "but I'm willing to admit there's a limit to my smartness."

"Y' don't say!"

Chip flushed darkly. "One thing I do know. I can get in there and find out how many men they've got, and when they're going to open the ball, and how. And I can get out again. Looks to me," he added sharply, "as if that's pretty damned vital information. But, of course, being only about half-witted, that's just my fool notion."

"Don't be a daw-gone chump," growled J.G. "You better take somebuddy along with yuh, if you're hell-bent on goin'."

Having gained his point, Chip stood up. "I don't want anyone. Two'll make just twice as much stir outside as one. Moreover, I can hear as much as two, and if I don't get back—"

"If you don't get back outa there," said J.G., also on his feet now, "if they glom yuh, we won't know no more'n we do now what's going on."

"If I don't get back," Chip repeated steadily, "they'll

know the Flying U is wise to them, and you'll have to move quick. You'll need every man you've got." He lifted his hat, resettled it on his head, pulling it low on his forehead for hard riding. "I'll be back, though. You can look for me at the Hobble-O sometime between midnight and daylight. All depends on how long-winded they are down there."

"A gov'ment mule's got nothin' on you for stubbornness," J.G. observed dissatisfiedly, but the look in his eyes belied the criticism. "You're takin' the bit in your teeth—"

"Well, I've kept all four feet under me so far."

The older man walked to the door, looked out at the men roosting on the corral fence just down the slope, turned and came to a stand beside Chip. He took his pipe from his mouth, looked into the bowl as if the ashes held the words he wanted.

"I'm a daw-gone fool," he said savagely. "I'd oughta let yuh go get yourself in a jackpot and git out the best way you can. Or let you take your medicine and scratch your name off'n the payroll. But damn it, Chip, I knowed your folks and I knowed you when you wasn't knee-high to a grasshopper. You ain't got anybody but me to ride herd on yuh and—daw-gone it—"

Chip did a most unusual thing, one he would have called silly at another time less freighted with anxiety. He lifted a hand and laid it across J.G.'s shoulder as though this was his father or his brother, worried over the danger he wanted to face.

"I know," he said softly. "Same here, J.G. You've

been more like a daddy than a boss. I guess we both know about how we stack up to each other." He paused, drawing in his breath with a faint sigh.

"You're like my own kid—if I'd ever had one," J.G. muttered fretfully.

"And I've got to go and get the facts down there, because—it's *you* they're planning to wipe out. You and your outfit." His hand slid away from the other as he moved toward the door. "It'll save argument with some of the boys if you call them all up here for a talk," he said in his ordinary, matter of fact tone. "Just as well if I don't have the whole bunch next to what I'm going to do."

J.G. looked at him, gave a grudging nod. Chip was ten feet from the door when the final word came. "If you ain't showed up at the Hobble-O by the first crack of dawn, we'll be down there after yuh. And God help 'em, if we do that!" he added half to himself.

Over his shoulder Chip sent him a quick boyish smile. "I'll be drifting in sometime after midnight—and if I don't have the deadwood on that bunch, it'll be because their mouths are riveted shut and they can't talk. You can bank on that, old-timer."

After a full twelve hours of sleep, he walked with the stilted stride of high-heeled riding boots, his shoulders back and the air of assurance conjured by his words. At the bunkhouse door he paused to shout down to the corral:

"Hey, you fellows! Get a move on, down there! J.G. wants to see you."

"All of us?" Shorty called back, as he and some

others slid down off the fence, more getting up from the ground and brushing down their pants with the flat of their palms.

"Yeah, the whole bunch," Chip yelled, and went into the cabin to wait, while all the footsteps went trooping past. When the last soft thudding sound receded up the path, he came out again, his rifle lying in the crook of his arm.

XXIV
POLLY PLAYS LADY

THE TWO WOMEN OF THE HOBBLE-O WERE BUSY IN the kitchen when Jim Whitmore knocked at the door. Or, to be exact, Polly was busy making dried-apple pies, and her mother was hushing her fretful yearling on her shoulder, in the hope of persuading him to sit on the floor with a tin pan and big iron spoon and bang it happily, so that she might "look over" a mess of beans and get them to parboiling. The other youngsters had long since been taught to keep out from underfoot and were playing upstairs.

With her free hand, Mrs. Taylor pulled open the door and smiled welcome. "Well, come right in! Shep's been askin' for you and worryin' because you didn't show up this mornin' bright and early. Seems—uh—how-de-do?" she finished with vague politeness, seeing that the big, lumbering fellow with the Dutch face and a sagging paunch was coming in behind Whitmore.

"Mis' Taylor, I brought my round-up cook along to

take a hold here and give you women a breathin' spell," J.G. answered her look of inquiry. "Patsy by name—and a cookin' fool. The rest of the boys and about a dozen more'll be along perty soon, and there's a pack-load er two of grub on the way. We're makin' this our headquarters for the time bein'. You women folks clear out now and roll down your sleeves. Patsy'll handle the kitchen while the crowd's here."

"You pet my life," grinned Patsy. "Cooking for hungry punchers iss my yob, alreatty. You go set down and rest yourself, Mis' Taylor. I cook you goot grub, by colly."

"You bet your boots he will, Mom. I had some of his cooking and I know," Polly declared, brushing flour from her rounded arms. "Well, here's the piecrust and filling all ready for you, Patsy. Fly at it. I'm going to play lady from now on."

Though she laughed when she said it, her eyes turned anxiously to the window. "Did—did all the boys come down with you, Mr. Whitmore?" she asked, in what she believed a casual tone. "I—suppose they'll all be here for supper."

"Yeah, most of 'em, I guess. All but Chip. Well, maybe I better not bother Shep right now, Mis' Taylor—not if he's asleep or anything—"

"Land, he ain't slept a wink and he won't, till he's had a chance to talk things over with you. The man's about distracted, bein' laid up at a time like this. Come on in and see him. It'll do him a sight more good than layin' there frettin' and worryin'."

But Polly forestalled her. "You go take the baby and lie down, Ma, and maybe he'll go to sleep. I'll take Mr. Whitmore in to see Dad." And though her mother refused the luxury of lying down in the daytime, she did yield to the extent of resting in the big old-fashioned rocker, holding the baby on her lap and hushing his fretful whimpering.

So Polly had her chance to listen while the two men talked. It was not until J.G. had finished, however, that she had anything to say.

"I believe I know where that secret trail leaves Goodwater Canyon, Mr. Whitmore. I should think you'd want to have some of your men there, ready to start action the minute Butch makes a move. He must have a lot more men than we have, and if he once gets out of Fishback on the warpath—"

"Well, Chip's goin' to find out how many men he's got and what-all he figures on doin'," J.G. patiently explained. "There ain't been anything but talk, so fur. We've got to have something we can get our teeth in. No use goin' off half-cocked and mebby findin' ourselves outside the law."

"No, we can't break the law just because they do," Shep agreed. "Whitmore's right. We're forewarned and that's somethin'."

"And in the meantime, if Chip gets caught—and you don't find out any more—I suppose you'll still go on waiting!" Polly's breath was suddenly uneven, her eyes suspiciously inclined to blink.

Jim Whitmore's hands, resting in his spread knees, closed slowly into fists. "If Chip ain't showed up here by three in the morning, we'll be down there after him," he said grimly.

"A lot of good that'll do him!"

"Well, he claimed there ain't any risk at all, skurcely. He said he'd wait till about dark and then git in back of the house and listen by a window that's got a hole in the glass. He said there wasn't one chance in a hundred anybody would spot him, and if they did, he'd git away in the brush, back out the way he got in. I guess he's safe enough. It'll give us a line on that bunch, so if they do aim to start anything, we can beat 'em to it. Chip ain't nobody's fool. He'll make out all right." He was talking to reassure himself, for he added, "Chip'll git in there and git out again if anybody can do it. He's like his dad was at his age. There ain't much gits past him."

"Well, of course, they'll only be about forty or fifty against one, if they do nab him. He won't mind a little thing like that." Polly's chin went up in the gesture Chip knew so well. "Still—he isn't invulnerable, you know."

"No, and he ain't goin' to be!" Shep fretfully declared from his pillow. "I'd back that boy anywhere. Quit your fussin', Polly, and go tell your ma I want her."

"Well, all right," Polly yielded with surprising docility and departed on her errand.

Her mother was just laying the baby down asleep, s-sh-ing and patting his limp little body as she withdrew her hand carefully from under him. Polly waited until the old brown shawl had been drawn up over him, then plucked her mother's sleeve and led her across the room.

"I'm going to take a ride," she announced, when she had delivered the message. "For goodness' sake don't tell Pa, or he'll have a fit. It's safe enough, with all these men around and more coming. I've got to get outside. And don't go worrying—"

"Where you headed for now?" Ma Taylor's voice, though discreetly lowered, carried strong disapproval. "I can't have you stramming around the country and maybe getting yourself shot—"

"Oh, for pity's sake, Ma! There's more danger right here at home, far as that goes, and it certainly is safe enough here. I'm just going to meet Chip, but I may be gone quite a while, persuading him to have some sense and come on in and behave himself."

"Ain't he with the rest of the boys?"

"No, he's—flocking off by himself, as usual. I—we had a fight and he's just stubborn. I'm going to try and talk some sense into him, that's all."

"Well," sighed her mother, "Chip's a peculiar boy; a very peculiar boy. You shouldn't talk to him the way you do, Polly. You know he's like a high-spirited horse—he won't stand for being beat over the head. He's proud—"

"Beat over the head!" sniffed Polly. "That's something I never tried yet. It might work. Anyway, don't tell folks where I've gone, will you, Mommy? Just say I'm upstairs with the toothache or something. If the boys ever got hold of the fact I've gone after Chip—Well, you know."

"I should think you would be ashamed of it," her mother observed tartly. "If you treated him like a human being, you wouldn't have to. You better eat humble pie for once in your life, honey, and get that boy back here where he belongs. And don't forget your rifle, and don't wait to ask questions if you see any strangers prowlin' around. All the law-abidin' men in the country are either here on the ranch or they're comin'. Them that ain't is in cahoots with Milt and Big Butch. So act according."

"I will, Mother. You're sure a brick, do you know that?" And Polly flew to change her clothes, while her deluded parent went unsuspectingly to assemble doughnuts and meaty sandwiches in a generous package, on the theory that Polly might find the way to soften Chip's pride by tempting his stomach.

Indeed, Ma Taylor admitted it, when she intercepted Polly on the way out. "You take this. You can ketch more flies with sugar than you can with vinegar, and the poor boy's most likely half starved for good victuals and wouldn't own it."

"I'm not out to catch flies or anything else, Ma. I'll tell him you sent it. Don't say anything now, will you?"

"I ain't likely to. If I didn't know you're as capable with a gun as your father, and have got about as much sense, I wouldn't let you stir a step away from the place. But I do think Chip oughta be persuaded to come in with the rest of the boys and not hang off by himself like this. Well—you git back as quick as you can, Polly."

"I will, Ma."

With her rifle under her arm and her sour-dough coat buttoned under her chin, she would have passed as one of the boys, had any of the strangers seen her go. But the boys, Harvey and Ernest, were busily trailing beef rustlers in a thicket across the coulee and arguing hotly over clues, as their distant voices testified. The men were keeping inside today and a hard-fought game of penny ante was going on in the bunkhouse. No one noticed Polly as she walked past the window, on her way to the stable.

Riding out of the coulee past the guard stationed behind a rocky hummock gave her a few uneasy moments, but she was careful not to hurry too much and she whistled as she rode and looked like a boy on some simple errand, so the guard merely stared and let her go. Once away from the coulee, she turned into the hills and was lost to sight.

And this was the way in which Polly played lady that afternoon: With her rifle across the saddle in front of her and her eyes watching everything—but mostly the keen wise ears of her brown horse Pathfinder—she headed for the canyon she called Goodwater, taking every shortcut trail she knew—and you may believe that Polly knew them all. And so, riding fast as the roughness of the country would permit, she reached the canyon and followed it to the sandy wash where a single line of vague prints, like horse tracks weeks old, pointed the way for her.

Those tracks were fresher than they looked, as Polly well knew by certain other signs and by her own shrewd reasoning. Chip had ridden that trail not twenty minutes before, though she did not know this, but could only guess that he had already come this way. He had started early in the afternoon, J.G. had said; and while he would have ridden cautiously, keeping off the sky line of ridges and following the devious course of certain lateral canyons and gulches little frequented and making time-eating detours, by now he must have reached this point.

And what if outlaws out to the eastward, those accomplices who had received and marketed the beef for Milt, had been bidden to this devil's assembly tonight? The blood drained from Polly's cheeks when she thought of Chip running into them in some narrow trap of a gulch. But then she thought they would probably ride first to the Lazy Ladder and come over with Milt, and her breath eased a little. Perhaps, after all, he would make it safely through.

Of herself, her own danger, she scarcely thought at all. Or if she did, it was impersonally, wishing she had had the time to fix boots for Pathfinder so his hoofprints in the wash would not so blatantly advertise the passing of a stranger. And she told herself that even if she met someone, she would not be shot on sight. She'd just make the timeworn excuse that she was hunting stray horses—something like that. Be wide-eyed and innocent, suspecting nothing. No one would hurt her—she could shoot as straight as any of them, if it came to that. But Chip—they were out to get him; kill him on sight. It was a crazy thing to do, riding right in to listen under Butch's window. Crazier even than when he had gone to Butch before and accused him of butchering other people's cattle. Then he had a chance. Now he knew he'd be killed if they caught him.

It would serve him right, she told herself fiercely. She wasn't thinking of him, it was her father and mother and the kids she was worried about. And all the decent people north of the river. Why, those nesters had families, some of them. Let Butch and Milt have their way, and a dozen homes would be ravaged, women and children left to starve, probably, because their menfolks were gone.

Of course it wasn't Chip! It was just that he would probably be killed, and someone had to know what was going on down here. That was all in the world that had brought her. Only for that, she would have stayed at home.

This being the case, she rode warily, careful to take no wrong turning, following those blurred marks where they showed. And the soft purple shadows flowed down the eastern slopes into the deep gorges where she must ride, and her heart and her throat felt as if they were caught in a vise. But she kept on going, and so long as she could see Pathfinder's ears, she knew that she would have warning of danger. And she strained her ears for the sound of gunshots and counted each minute of that eerie silence as something precious, since it spelled safety for that time at least.

XXV

AT BUTCH'S WINDOW

Already darkness was creeping in upon Chip, so that only his memory of that obscure and crooked trail held him from going astray and losing himself in those labyrinthine gorges; though Mike too remembered and took the right turns unerringly. In the last narrow gulch Chip dismounted, tied the horse behind a clump of bushes and went on afoot, walking carefully, his spurs hung over the saddle horn, lest the chains betray him with their clinking against rocks.

His rifle, too, was in its scabbard on the saddle. He did not need it now—indeed, it would only be a handicap. If it came to fighting, he'd want his hands free, and he had his dad's old forty-five with its steer-head butt. If that wouldn't pull him out of this, nothing would, he thought, as he slipped along, his left hand touching the rock wall, his right ungloved and swinging free.

Tonight he did not climb the side wall, but kept straight on; though not straight, either, since there were three distinct turns, like crooked elbows, before he saw the blotchy shadows of trees just ahead. Here he waited, listening and straining eyes to see. The brush hid everything from view, however, even in daylight, and there were no tangible sounds save the wind rustling bare branches in the thicket. There was nothing to be gained by waiting there and he moved on into the blackness of the grove.

It was well that he did. He was no more than a few rods from the narrow entrance when from behind him he heard voices muttering indistinctly, Milt Cummings' pleasing tones rising distinct above the others. While he shrank down against a thick young pine, they rode by so close he could have whispered and made them hear. So close that horses shied away from him and were cursed for their skittishness.

"Bet we're late," said one; and Milt's voice answered him arrogantly:

"No, we ain't late. Time to start is when we get there, and don't you forgit it. They can't open the ball without us."

Another voice spoke and someone else said, "Cut it out. We're there."

Then, out beyond the little grove, Big Butch called out, "That you, Milt?"

"Sure it's me," Milt called back. "Me and twelve more—good men and true."

"Well, put up your horses and git in here. The sooner we git started, the quicker."

When they were gone, Chip lifted himself carefully away from the little pine and felt his way again toward the cabin, taking slow steps, stopping each time to listen. Once he was almost certain that he heard someone behind him, and he froze to attention, face turned toward the cleft. He did not hear the sound again, though he waited some minutes, his gun in his hand.

He was just relaxing, convinced that his imagination had made footsteps out of the whisper and rasp of the wind in the grove, when a shadow eased away from blacker shade and drifted silently toward him. On the nape of Chip's neck the skin tightened. His gun arm came up and back, ready for the smashing blow that would lay the fellow out and still avoid rousing the place with a shot. His eyes narrowed, gleamed ruthless in the dark.

Nearer that vague shape moved, and then—"Chip!" A breathless pause, and "Chip! It's me—Polly!" All in a whisper no louder than the sough of the slow wind through the thicket of young pines.

Chip's knees buckled. He found himself shaking, his strength gone. Had he walked, he would have staggered, but he stood still, making a soft hushing sound like the hiss of a snake. As she came up to him, he reached out and pulled her close against his trembling body.

"Go back!" he breathed peremptorily as he bent. "For godsake, what are you doing here? Who's with you?"

Polly leaned within the circle of his arm and lifted herself on her toes to reach his ear. "I'm alone. I came because—you mustn't be here by yourself. If anything happened—"

"You'll have to go back. You must be crazy." He holstered his gun, furiously trying to think what to do now. "We're within fifty feet of the cabin. Get out of here before somebody sees you. It wouldn't be so funny this time if they caught you."

"They won't. I'm going to stay with you. I—I'm scared to go back now, Chip. A whole bunch of men came along just as I had tied Pathfinder alongside Mike. I was simply paralyzed! I had to scrooch in against the wall in a kind of niche or they'd have seen me sure. What if I met somebody on the way back out?"

"Serve you damn right." So far as it is possible to show anger and disgust in a whisper, Chip crowded them in. "Stay here then. I've got to get the low-down on this bunch. And, for the lordsake, keep your nose out of this!"

To that Polly made no reply. He thought she was crying—which she was not—and he released her, admonished her again to stand right there and try and have some sense, and went on, making his way cautiously toward the rough low muttering of many voices speaking at once, after the manner of men waiting for a speaker to begin.

The window he had mentioned revealed itself as a square of dim yellow in the surrounding darkness. Chip edged up to the cabin corner, flattening himself against the rough log wall and inched along until the window was just ahead. The hum of talk was louder now, brutish laughter riding the uneven waves of sound. Evidently the conference had not yet started, perhaps because all had not yet arrived. Two or three were enjoying themselves hugely at the expense of one they called Owley, whose horse had piled him that afternoon. There was plenty of swearing and ribald witticisms—stock phrases among ranchmen which Chip was thankful Polly was not there to hear.

And then he discovered her close behind him and

dared not tell her what he thought of her. She reached out and twitched his coat until he bent his head to hear what she had to say.

"Have they started?" she breathed close to his face, and Chip was forced to whisper "No!" with his lips almost touching her cheek. And he added, "Go back!"

"No!" whispered Polly, and Chip could have shaken her.

No use to argue the point, though. She was there and he couldn't do anything about it. Whispering outside Big Butch's window was not exactly a safe thing to do, once that bunch in there stopped laughing at Owley and quieted down. Lucky for them, there was a wind rustling the branches; that made it easier to get away with this. But if little Polly didn't keep still . . .

Polly did, though, and Chip's thoughts were diverted by a hail down toward the corral. Instantly the talk and laughter in the cabin ceased. He risked a glance inside, guessing that all eyes would be turned toward the door which stood in the other wall—the one facing south. This window looked east, away from the corral which was to the west.

"It's the Cow Island boys," a man leaned in the doorway to announce, and there was a general stir, a shuffling of boots on the plank floor.

Chip had never seen a room so full of men. They were standing—there was no room to sit down. The cabin was built to accommodate ten or a dozen men at a pinch. There must be at least three times that many and more were coming. He heard them walking up the path, their footsteps plainly audible on the freezing ground. There were brief greetings as the crowd shifted to let them in.

"All set?" Big Butch's voice was lifted, dominating the room.

"All set," several answered here and there about the room.

"Well, you know what we're here for, I guess," Butch began. "We've thrashed it out pretty thorough in the last few months. We need more territory and we're out to get it in the only way it can be got. This is a great country—a damn sight too good to let a bunch of mossback farmers and a couple of cowmen glom it all. This is horse country—"

"You said it," someone filled the pause he made, and there were muttered affirmations throughout the room.

"Well, no use goin' into all that, I guess. You boys was got together here to git your last instructions, before you kinda scatter out and git to work. But things has changed some. There ain't goin' to be no scatterin', boys. We got to git action and git it quick."

"That's the stuff, Butch!" a loud voice unctuously approved. "Now you're talkin'."

"Why the sudden change uh heart, Butch?" Milt Cummings demanded in his most sarcastic tone. "Way you bawled me out for tryin' to speed things up a little—hell, I thought you was goin' to wait and let Shep Taylor and Jim Whitmore die of old age!"

"You thought nothin' of the kind, Milt. You took the bit in your teeth the other night and damn near spilled the hull works and I called yuh on it. This thing has got to be handled right or we're going to be in the soup. And at the same time, some things have come up today that I don't like the looks of none too well. Looks like our hand is liable to be forced."

"Meanin' what?" From the sounds, Chip guessed that Milt was pushing in closer to Butch. "Who's forcin' our hand, Butch?"

"Well, Blink Roberts never showed up today, like he was s'posed to, for one thing. Him and Shep Taylor and the Bennett kid, they left the ranch 'long about dusk yesterday, and nothin's been seen of 'em since. And then today, the high mucky-muck of the Flyin' U rides over to the Hobble-O—him and three-four fellows Sam didn't seem able to place. And they ain't left yet; or they hadn't, a couple of hours ago. The girl rode off alone, though—back in the hills somewhere. Too much ridin' back and forth to suit me."

"Jest millin' around, chewin' the rag, most likely," a new voice commented. "Prob'ly don't mean nothin' much."

"Mebby not. Then agin it might mean a damn sight too much. Git Jim Whitmore and Old Shep Taylor together, and I wouldn't put nothin' past 'em. They ain't got no time for me, never had. It's only a matter of just so long till they try an' frame something on me and my outfit. Prob'ly cookin' up somethin' right now."

There were mutterings and a restless stirring within the room. Strange voices spoke stranger sentiments. Standing outside that window, Chip—Polly, too, since she could not help hearing—listened to an amazing discussion of ethics. They heard that the Hobble-O, the Flying U and all the nesters in the country were range hogs, grabbing right and left and always looking for a chance to give these men a raw deal.

The country had to be cleaned up, no doubt about that; and the sooner it was done, the quicker Butch and his friends would prosper. Why, look how they had crowded Butch down into these canyons! Could he range a decent bunch of horses? He could not. A hundred head was his limit, just about. Why, he could hardly hold a horse long enough for the brand to heal, much less hair over. Had to monkey around so much fixing brands there wasn't a dollar a head profit any more, hardly.

It was all because of their neighbors. They made that very plain to themselves and to one another; also that they had no recourse save to protect their own interests. Hearing them talk, a stranger would have thought that these were the law-abiding men, banding together to rid the country of a bunch of dangerous outlaws.

Then Butch once more took the floor. Apparently he had let them talk so that he could gauge anew their temper. His plans were settled long ago in his own mind and he was ready now to give them out.

"We're ready to start and there ain't any use waitin'," he declared, lifting his voice so that it carried to the men grouped outside the door. "We hit for the Hobble-O first, glom their guard—my boys know where he hangs out at the mouth of the coulee—and go in and round up what men's there. Blink's job was to jim all the guns he could git his hands on, workin' at night. If he's done his work, there ain't goin' to be much trouble.

"Work quiet as you can. We don't want to croak any women if we can help it—"

"We'll take care uh the women!" someone by the door shouted coarsely and laughed afterwards.

"If we work it right, the women won't know what's takin' place," Butch ignored the interruption. "We don't want to git in bad, and botherin' women folks sure raises hell all around. We take the Hobble-O delegation right along with us—"

"Alive?"

"Well," Butch said dryly, "live men rides better than dead ones and there won't be no saddles to clean. Sure, alive, if we c'n handle 'em. We drift over to the Flyin' U and ketch 'em bedded down. Make a clean-up there, d'yuh see? And we leave them Hobble-O fellers layin' around artistic, right where they fell—to show who it was jumped the Flyin' U and what happened to 'em. Then we go round up the nesters, as many as we can git our hands on, and pack 'em back to the Flyin' U for evidence they was in on it too."

"That's quite a contract for one night, Butch," Milt Cummings observed dubiously.

Butch gave a short laugh. "It ain't much of a contract for these boys here. Thirty miles of good road to the Flyin' U, and mebbe another twenty or twenty-five roundin' up the nesters. How about it, boys?"

"Pickin's," a young-sounding voice piped up, "if we don't have to lay in the bresh, swappin' lead with somebuddy for a hour or two on the way."

"Nothin' like that at the Hobble-O," Butch declared. "It'll be a case of ride in, glom every man in sight and ride out agin quiet. Might have to drag a gun off'n somebuddy's head to git him quiet—nothin' that had oughta take any time a-tall. Call old Shep down to the bunkhouse—all straight an' simple. If Blink's back, he'll be a big help gittin' old Shep outside. If he ain't, we'll work it some other way."

"What about the gitaway?"

"Got somethin' a hell of a sight better'n a gitaway. Here's Tom Shaner, right here. Tom, you sift on back and tell Barr and the rest we're settin' it ahead. It's tonight we're all in his place. Burch'll vouch fer that, all right. And if you've got the captain of the Vigilantes vouchin' for yuh," he laughed, "you don't need to worry about no gitaway! It's a dead immortal cinch."

"That's right too," the voice that had inquired assented in a relieved tone. "You're there with the goods, Butch."

"Hell, I've been all winter figurin' how we could git this range cleaned up," Butch modestly belittled his shrewdness. "Milt makin' that bobble with his lynchin' party kinda knocked my plan in the head, but I dunno as it makes much difference, in the long run. Long as we git the job done, the quicker the sooner, I guess."

Chip had heard enough and more than enough. He turned and put out a hand toward Polly, heard her gasp and stumble. A dead stick snapped with a cracking sound.

"Get outa here—quick!" he hissed in her ear, and pushed her toward the cabin corner, as a vague bulk showed ten feet away, coming from the listening knot of men before the door.

XXVI

POLLY PUTS IT OVER

"WHO'S THAT?" THE MAN HESITATED, TOOK A STEP forward and halted again, as if he were half convinced it were none of his business. "What's the matter?"

"Huh? Not a thing in the world." Chip's voice was rough and throaty as he answered. With a purely instinctive movement, he reached for a match, lighted it and cupped the blaze between his palms as he pretended to light a cigarette, half turned away from the wind and the stranger. While the glow did not reveal his face, it did convince the fellow that Chip had nothing to hide. "Got a grand-stand seat here," he added, carelessly turning back to the window, as the match dropped and he set his foot upon it.

With a careless hand he beckoned. "You can see and hear a damn sight better than with that bunch milling around by the door," he muttered. "Come and take a look."

Without hesitation, the man approached. One of the new men from Wyoming, probably. Certainly he was a stranger to Chip. As he lifted a hand and set it against the wall, leaning and peering in through the round hole in the glass, the temptation to bring his gun barrel down over the fellow's head was almost irresistible to Chip. His fingers itched to lay the man cold where he stood.

But that would only invite trouble. Someone might hear the fall—they would be almost certain to discover him later and know that an enemy had been in camp.

Inside the cabin voices were growing louder. Butch and Milt Cummings had locked horns in acrimonious argument over the feasibilities of accomplishing so thorough a clean-up in one night. What if the Hobble-O put up a fight? How were they going to make it appear to the world afterwards that Shep Taylor had gone over to fight the Flying U? What if they didn't locate all the nesters? There were a lot of women—four or five, anyway—that would holler their heads off. Butch was plumb loco if he thought he could go hog-wild like that and get away with it.

This and more held the man to the window. And because there seemed some doubt of the outcome, Chip stayed, looking over the shoulder of the other. A strange and touchy situation, and one that would have amazed those inside had they been aware of it.

Big Butch with his imported outlaws easily dominated the situation. Crazy as the scheme looked, the crowd was plainly for it, and by its very audacity it might succeed; or would if they could catch their victims unprepared.

The moment Milt gave ground and Butch began issuing his orders, appointing his leaders—so many men for the kidnapping, certain others for the round-up of the nesters, another group who would be responsible for all temporary prisoners—Chip began to edge away. He was behind a tree and out of sight when the man at the window missed him and turned to see where he had gone. From the black shadows he watched the fellow crane and look, and when he started toward the front of the cabin, Chip moved on to the next tree and the next, wary as a wolf and nearly as noiseless.

But when the sounds of departure indicated a general exodus from the cabin, Chip ran as if they were all after him hot-foot. Within the blackness of the gorge he went stumbling along, heedless of the noise he made. Unless they entered the narrow twisting gorge they wouldn't hear him, and if they were after him, the noise wouldn't matter; they'd know he was ahead of them, anyway.

When he reached Mike, he paused a moment to listen. There was no sound save the soft whooing of the wind overhead and the beat of his own blood in his ears. With his knife he slashed the thongs that held the cowhide on Mike's feet—no need of that precaution now—mounted and started at a breakneck pace down the trail.

How long it would take that outlaw army to reach the Hobble-O he could only guess, but his guessing increased his apprehension. Unless they took longer than usual to get under way, they'd be at the Hobble-O in a couple of hours. He'd have to beat their speed. Following these damned gulches and canyons would lose time for him; he knew of no shortcuts to the big canyon. Impossible to make it in less than two hours and yet it had to be done.

Oddly, he forgot just how much Polly had heard before he sent her away. He was under the impression that she had stepped on that stick when Butch was justifying himself and his ideas to his men, and that she knew nothing of their plan to move in on the Hobble-O that night. She had taken Pathfinder and gone home—or at least she had started. But she wouldn't know how urgent it was and she would probably fool along, waiting for him to overtake her.

Mike knew the trail. If he hadn't, he never could have taken the turns the way he did, snaking around sharp corners of rock, tobogganing down steep little slides where before he had picked his way with cow-pony caution. In those gorges the night was pitch black, but Chip scarcely gave it a thought. He was going to overtake Polly before Big Butch's gang came up with her. On the last mile or two they would travel the same road.

For the next half hour or more the way was rough. Mike smoothed it with his unfaltering stride. He knew this country. He had a memory of the stretches where a horse could easily break a leg if he were not careful and put them behind him as fast as he came up with them. There were places too where his master often turned aside into some box canyon or some brushy draw—places Mike remembered perfectly and passed by tonight, as if he knew that something much more vital than nosing into out-of-way places was required of him.

Where the way opened to the Devil's Dipper, he

slowed a little, not quite certain whether they might be making for that little meadow. A sharp dig of the spurs told him to keep going. He went. The Hobble-O Ranch then; it was the only other place where his master had gone in a hurry lately, and Mike tucked his ears back flat against his head and ran belly to the ground. Whatever was in the wind, he certainly meant to do his part. He'd give all he had, any day, if this master of his wanted and needed it.

Chip did. With the back of his mind he knew that he was getting it. He had no quarrel with Mike, yet the pace seemed maddeningly slow. He kept seeing Polly as she had looked, a vague little figure there in the dusk among the trees. No business to be there—crazy thing for a girl to do. Haze off down to an outlaw camp like Big Butch's, when she knew he had a big gang there making war medicine—just to find out what they were up to!

But he knew better than that, even while he thought it; he knew that was not the reason she went. She went because she knew he had gone, and she had the crazy idea that maybe she could help him somehow; the same crazy idea that had put her down in Fishback canyon with her rifle, ready to fight the whole outfit if she saw he was getting the worst of it.

And now she'd hang back and wait for him to come along, and if he didn't show up when she thought he should, it would be just like her to turn around and come looking for him, even if she had to go in and drag him out of Big Butch's cabin. He wouldn't put it past her. She didn't have a lick of sense about dodging danger, that girl.

Mike slowed for a ridge he must climb over. Wet to the tip of his ears, he still planted his feet with a sureness that carried him steadily up to the top and down the steep slope beyond. His muscles worked smoothly, his breathing was strong and not too fast. He was what is called a stayer—he had need to be, to carry young Chip Bennett along some of the trails he chose to ride.

As he came out into the narrow valley which formed the one connecting link between the Hobble-O and that rough country where Big Butch had his stronghold, and farther along opened into Lazy Ladder country, Chip pulled Mike down to a walk. The horse needed the breathing spell, but also the slower pace gave a chance to listen. Here, if anywhere along the trail, he would get some evidence of whether he was too late.

Dust hung in the air. He could smell it, or at least he imagined that he could. Whether it was the dust of Polly's crossing, or Butch's men, or both, he of course could not tell. Even the wind might have swept it up into the air. And then he resorted to an Indian trick. He dismounted, knelt and laid an ear against the ground. Instantly he knew they were coming—or were they going? Unmistakably there was the beat of galloping hoofs, like the distant throb of a small herd running; or of cavalry. The direction, however, he could not determine. They might have passed this point already or they might be coming. He couldn't wait there to find out, that was certain. All he could do was go on and trust to luck.

At least he knew now that Polly was somewhere ahead of him, and as he tore along the trail, he tried to convince himself that Butch's gang was behind him; that he rode between them and the girl. He'd come up with her pretty quick now, he was sure of that. She hadn't hung back so much waiting for him, he thought, with a perverse sense of resentment. A lot she must have cared, after all, beating it like that without waiting to see what kind of a jackpot she had got him into! He'd have something to say on the subject when he caught up with her. The way he'd haze her home wouldn't be slow—fooling along when that devil of a Butch Lewis was on the war-path. . . .

He caught up with Polly sooner than he expected. Rather, he met her coming headlong down the trail, lunging at him from the dark. Their horses swung wide to avoid a collision, for they met at a bend in the road. With one impulse they pulled up and reined around, meeting face to face.

"Hey, where you think you're going now?" Chip cried sharply. "Don't you know—"

"Oh, you got away!" gasped Polly. "I've been so worried—but I had to go and warn J.G. and the boys. That's what you wanted, wasn't it? But I sneaked away and came back as fast as I could, Chip. I was so afraid—"

"You warned them? Did you hear what Butch framed up to do tonight, I thought I chased you off before he spilled his plan."

"Of course I heard. I hope you don't flatter yourself I went to please you? Somebody had to get to the ranch and tell the boys what was going to come off tonight, didn't they? It certainly didn't look as if you were going to leave in a hurry, so I hustled home and told them what to expect."

"You sure must have flown."

"I'm riding a *horse,*" Polly told him significantly. "Besides. I happen to know all the shortcuts. I didn't have to wander up and down all the canyons that happened to hold an outlaw sign—I make time when I want to."

"You sure had better show a sample of speed now, if it's so simple. That bunch is coming somewhere behind us, and not so far behind either, if you ask me. Clear out. Take your darned shortcuts and go home."

"There aren't any, from here on," Polly admitted. "Why don't you show a little speed yourself, if they're so close? I don't notice you tearing any bones out hurrying."

In the starlight he looked at her loping along beside him, a gallant little figure on a horse whose stiffened gait betrayed how tired he was. Mike, too, had used his best effort and galloped heavily; a grunt jarred from him with every leap he took.

Chip looked again at Polly. What shone in his eyes the darkness hid well. His voice was as gruff as he could make it. "A man's supposed to ride between a lady and harm. Kick that crowbait out of a walk and make yourself scarce around here, or it'll take more than my natural chivalry to keep lead from coming your way."

"Sorry, but my horse can't travel one bit faster than yours."

"He'd sure travel if I had the handling of him," Chip stated grimly. "Don't be a darned chump—get going, why don't you?"

"Well, why don't you get going yourself? You're not bullet proof, you know."

"Because Mike's given all he's got, that's why," Chip told her bluntly. "He'll go till he drops, but there's no use crowding him—he's doing his darnedest right now."

"You just want to be ornery and hang back and pick a fight. You may call that chivalry, but I've got another name for it."

Chip was riding half turned in the saddle, listening. "You hear that? They'll be on top of us in a minute or two."

"Yes, I hear," said Polly in a squeezed, too quiet tone.

"Well, get a move on! Good Lord, don't you know what'll happen, if they ride up on you?"

"On us, you mean. Yes—I know. They—they won't tackle two as quick as one, and—"

"There's forty men coming, if there is one. Polly, go!"

"And one of the men is Milt Cummings, just aching to get a chance at you. No, I won't go."

"Well, come on, then! Throw the spurs into that old pelter and come on!"

The new burst of speed roweled from their horses lasted to the next little hill. Both jolted to a walk halfway up; Mike because he could gallop no farther just then, Pathfinder because Polly's hand was firm on the reins. She hoped Chip had not noticed it and she stole a look at him to make sure. Evidently he had not. He was twisted in the saddle again, staring back down the road as he listened.

Behind them the drumming of many hoofs sounded closer, yet not with any increase of tempo that would indicate pursuit. Big Butch had set himself and his men a hard ride for that night, and although fresh horses had been furnished for the work—good horses stolen from ranches off to the eastward of the Larb Hills—Butch was not setting too fast a pace. Probably he was even holding them back a little, wanting to give the Hobble-O time to settle down for the night. Certainly they had no suspicion that Chip and Polly rode a scant quarter of a mile ahead; the night was too dark and they themselves were making too much noise for that. But at the steady lope they were keeping, they must soon overtake the two. When that happened . . .

Each of them knew the answer very well. As they passed over the brow of the hill and Mike lifted himself into a trot down the farther slope, Chip turned his head and looked sharply at the girl.

"Mike's all in because I rode him down from the Flying U this afternoon—and missed all the low places in the road, getting to Butch's hangout. Then I certainly burned up the trail getting over here. And I didn't know any shortcuts." He put some sarcasm into that last statement.

"Well, I know it isn't his fault he has a hard master."

"But there's no excuse for that cayuse of yours," he

went on sternly. "Riding him down to Butch's and back shouldn't faze him. He's hard. The way you put him over these hills, he's got the wind of a mountain sheep. I think you're stalling. He isn't as played out as you're trying to let on. So—get going!"

Before she realized his purpose, Chip snatched his quirt off the saddle horn and gave the unsuspecting Pathfinder two vicious cuts across the rump. "Now, damn it, *ride!*" he gritted, and watched the horse go pounding off down the road, Mike valiantly trying to keep up.

XXVII

A CHINOOK STRIKES CHIP

A MILE AWAY YAWNED THE MOUTH OF HOBBLE-O Coulee, its bold rock rim outlined against the stars. Half a mile farther, within those arms, thirty rifles full fed with ammunition grimly waited to do battle. With a fresh horse Chip would have cared nothing for those pounding hoofbeats behind him. Even now, as Mike slowed and dropped to a walk, he felt only a deep exultant satisfaction that he had sent Polly on to safety. Back there, with her beside him, he had been close to panic.

He had little hope of making the Hobble-O himself. Short as the distance was, he knew it was too long. There wasn't any more speed in Mike. He had given every ounce and now he was ready to drop. He was staggering as he walked, head drooping, all the fire, all the spirit, gone out of him.

With his lips pressed into a straight line, Chip slid off, led the horse down into a gravelly wash weed-grown along the edges, and pulled the saddle off. A loose horse—no one would give it a second glance as they passed by, even if it were seen. They weren't after horses tonight, he thought bitterly.

With his rifle swinging at his side, he set off along the wash, Mike too far gone even to lift his head and look. He had done what he hated like poison in other men—ridden a willing horse almost to death. In a good cause; in the best of causes. It could not lessen the hurt, for all that. But if he hadn't done it, Polly would have ridden straight into that gang. It took just that last effort of Mike's to put him ahead of Big Butch and be the first to meet Polly. So it was worth it. Even if Mike laid down there in his tracks and died, he had helped save Polly Taylor.

Well, he had done his part, he guessed, though he would like to take a crack at Big Butch. They weren't coming on so fast. He wasn't hearing any hoofbeats at all now. Probably Butch had pulled up to give his final orders, or maybe to argue something out with Milt. Or perhaps they figured they were hitting the Hobble-O ahead of time and were waiting a while. He might make it in ahead of them, after all.

In the road he made better time, swinging along with his rifle over his shoulder. Imperceptibly the black hulk of the coulee rim drew closer. He had made half the distance when a rider bore swiftly down upon him, coming from the Hobble-O. "*Darn* that Polly!" gritted Chip. But it was not Polly this time. It was Weary

Davidson, wheeling his horse in beside Chip.

"Pile on, feller—you sure picked yourself a poor night for a ramble!" He pulled a foot from the stirrup and Chip swung himself up behind the cantle.

"Polly get in all right?"

"Polly? Her? Say, wildcats is canary birds alongside that gal of yours right now. Mamma! I thought J.G. was due to lose all his whiskers when he put his foot down and wouldn't let nobody lend her a fresh horse and come back herself after yuh. I dunno, on my soul, what do you do to 'em, Chip—"

"Oh, shut up! Boys ready to give Butch a hot reception?"

"They sure are. Butch is going to find he's bit off more'n he can chaw. Got to hand it to yuh, boy—"

"You do your handing somewhere else. There's about forty men in Butch's crowd. You fellows don't want to overlook that."

"Say, we ain't overlookin' a damn thing. How far back are they, about?"

"Mile, maybe. They must have stopped, back there a ways, or they'd of been on top of us before now. I thought I heard them coming again just as you rode up."

"Well, let 'em come. You and Polly sure put a crimp in their calculations for 'em. We'd all admire to see 'em show up—I tell you those."

As they swung into the coulee, a voice challenged them from the shadows. "Hold on there! Who are yuh?"

"Mamma! Is that all the long your memory is

tonight, Pat Casey? You know darned well who I am. And seeing as how my horse is packin' double, you know Chip." Weary's tone was bantering.

"Shore, I know. Couldn't take a chance though, could I? I'm s'posed to make damn shore who comes into this coulee. You heard—"

"Yeah, I heard. Well, the sheep's all in the c'rell now, Pat. Next is wolves and they're runnin' in a pack tonight. Let 'em past and close up the gap."

"Shore. How fur back?"

"It ain't how far back, it's how close up, you want to be thinkin' about. Tip the boys off and keep both eyes peeled."

"I know all that." Pat snubbed him and silence closed in upon the rocks where he was hiding.

The two rode on, splashed through the creek and loped on up to the corral. Here no sound greeted them. The place seemed deserted. "But you can't most always tell," chuckled Weary, when Chip spoke of the quiet. "This same coulee's filled to the guards with dynamite and don't you forget it!"

He turned his horse still saddled and bridled into the corral, touched Chip on the shoulder. "We stick together from now on, feller. Down here a ways. J.G. says to try not hit any horses, if you can help. They ain't done anything, and anyway, they're prob'ly stole off some poor devil of a rancher."

It was the huge boulder beside the trail that sheltered the two finally—the one where Skelp had waited to pounce on Chip. Memory of that encounter brought something else to mind.

"Butch had lookouts up on the rim. What about them, Weary?"

"Them? Not a word of trouble outa either one. Some of us boys done an Injun act and sneaked up on 'em. One got gay and tried to fight the outfit, and kinda got the worst of it. That Sam feller, he managed to annex a chunk of lead through his gizzard, and he's up in the house, talkin' wild and scattering. Ma Taylor's fixed him up a damn sight better than he deserves. The other one only got what was comin' to him."

"Dead?"

"And then some."

Far down the coulee vague sounds betrayed the approach of riders; the muffled tread of horses walking in sandy gravel, the creak of saddle leather, the clink of bridle chains and spurs. Whispers of sound scarcely to be distinguished from the rustle of weed and bush in the wind.

"They're comin'," Weary murmured, as he shifted his position a little. "When they git up here, we cut lose."

They waited, fingers crooked on triggers, rifles looking down the road. "Think they're sneaking up on men asleep," Chip whispered. "We can't let them get to the house, Weary. There's Polly—and the kids and Shep in bed—"

"Sh-sh—"

A blurred mass of figures moved toward them, heads and shoulders outlined against the stars.

"Get busy, you fellows!" hissed a voice above them in the rocks, and a rifle flamed and crashed behind the two.

A dozen six-shooters answered, bullets flying wild, as the startled horses lunged backward on those behind. The roar of outlaw guns was met and matched as the hillside blossomed with momentary bursts of orange flame. In the road, men ripped out blistering oaths of astonishment and pain. Some went reeling from their saddles and were kicked or trampled as the horses were jerked this way and that, their riders wanting to get away from there and do it quickly.

"It's a trap!" yelled Big Butch. "Get back, boys! Damn it, get back outa here!" And as his thoughts righted themselves, "Get the horses back outa here and smoke the sons uh guns outa them rocks!"

"You're damn right it's a trap!" someone high above on the hillside yelled exultantly. "You ain't the only ones smart enough to set traps—" And the speaker's guns spoke a swift tattoo.

The raiders wheeled and fled down the coulee to safety, and threw themselves off their horses in a hurry to get back into the fight. While they milled about in the road, J.G.'s voice, trained to carry across a herd, boomed down to them from the dark of a piled boulder outcropping.

"Butch! Milt! We've got you going and coming! The coulee's blocked agin yuh—take my advice and surrender!"

"Go to hell!" Butch yelled defiance. "You can't buffalo this bunch—we've been dogged off the range long as we're goin' to be. Come out into the open and fight, if yuh ain't too yella!"

"Surrender!" roared J.G. "I give yuh fair warnin'."

Butch cursed him savagely, speaking rapid words to his men in between. A burst of gunfire from the bank of the creek where some had already taken refuge, ducking down into the weeds and brush while Big Butch made his war talk, answered the Flying U boss.

J.G.'s men, cached farther down near the coulee mouth, closed up on the outlaws, keeping to the rocks and shooting down at the gun flashes along the creek bank. Butch's men fired at the yellow spurt among the rocks. The horses, wiser than their riders, stampeded across the creek and followed the meadow fence up the coulee toward the corrals and quiet.

Then the strategy of Jim Whitmore brought a new element into the fight. Suddenly the two old haystacks just over the fence in the meadow flamed up with a shower of sparks. The road was bathed in orange glow. Against the brilliant light of the burning stacks the outlaws lay revealed to those above them.

"We got yuh, Butch! For the third and last time, surrender!" J.G.'s stentorian voice floated down the hill.

And, "I'll see you in hell first!" Big Butch shouted and took careful aim toward the voice. "Git 'em boys! That fire shows them up same as it does us!"

With a discordant chorus of yells, the outlaws left their flimsy shelter—which now was no shelter at all—and charged the hill. Some sprawled headlong. Some kept going and gained the shelter of the scattered boulders just above the road. And the fire played no favorites but starkly revealed the hiding places of thieves and honest men alike. But at least it forced the battle to a definite conclusion, which perhaps was what J.G. had in mind when he ordered those stacks fired by men stationed behind them for that purpose.

Surrounded, their superior strength cut down with ruthless determination by men fighting for their homes as well as their lives, still the outlaws fought like cornered wolves. And they took their toll and laid men groaning among the rocks, and some took lead to themselves and fell silent. But more of the outlaws dropped their hot rifles and crumpled down within their shelters.

Milt Cummings was one of these. When the battle was over, and the chastened outlaws stood grotesquely invoking the quiet stars, the Flying U boys came upon Milt lying on his back behind a rock, the dulled glow of the burned-out stacks shining on his green-gray eyes. Big Butch huddled over a bullet wound in his middle, sweating with the pain of it and savage as a shot grizzly. Of the rest remaining alive, some were sullen, others whined for leniency or made excuses, placing the blame on Big Butch, who had led them into it, they said. In short, the survivors behaved as their natures impelled them to do. They expected a lynching party to follow the fight. It was what would have happened had they been the victors.

"It's Fort Benton and a judge an' jury for you fellers," J.G. grimly assured them. "We're law-abidin' men and we don't kill, except when killin's forced upon us. Rustle ropes, boys, and tie 'em up so they'll stay tied. Come daylight, we'll haul 'em in and turn 'em over. Dead or alive, the sheriff's goin' to have a chance to look 'em over. Daw-gone 'em, they've got records a mile long, an' I'll bet money on it."

Heartsick at the senseless slaughter they had brought upon themselves—and upon honest men—Chip turned away and started for the house. Maybe they had it coming to them; of course they had. No need to waste pity on men born to be hanged or shot for the evil they did. But Ted Culver didn't have it coming, and he lay dead back there, waiting for a wagon to come down and haul him up to the ranch. And that old trapper with an outlaw bullet in his brain—he didn't have it coming, nor the nester whose woman was a widow and didn't know it yet. It was like a war. It *was* war; the senseless, cruel war of greed against honest labor. Necessary, maybe—but he hated it and everything pertaining to it.

He'd pull out and go where there wasn't so much of this damned fighting and killing. There must be some place. . . .

A sound beside the big boulder halted him in his tracks. Another one hurt—only it didn't sound just like that, either. It sounded . . .

"Polly! Good Lord, girl, what are you doing out here? Are you hurt? If you're hurt— Say, if they've hurt you, I'll go back down there and—" He had her in his arms, holding her close, saying crazy, tender things in a broken voice, half whispering, his cold, hard cheek against her soft one with the tears running down. "Polly girl, don't cry! Don't you know I—it kills me to hear you cry like that?"

Two men passed them at a trot and Chip was silent until their footsteps receded up the road. His hands caressed her cheek, her hair, stilling her sobs with the very tenderness of his touch. When they were quite alone again, he leaned and set his lips against her mouth. And he found it very sweet and comforting, sending warm waves of strength and courage to his heart, his brain, making him feel as though he could fight Big Butch and his gang alone, if only it would make little Polly Taylor smile again.

"It's—so horrible," she said at last. "They said some of the cowboys were k-killed—and I thought—maybe it was you!"

"Ted Culver," he told her gently. "Through the heart—he never knew what hit him. And they paid—half of them are down and the rest are prisoners. Milt Cummings got it—there sure has been a clean-up. It'll be a different country after this. And it was you, Polly . . ."

Lovers have much to say that might sound silly if it were printed in cold type. Those two ran true to form, talking of themselves and what they really had meant when they quarreled, and what each thought the other had meant, and why. When they walked on up to the house, Chip's arm was around her—that much may go on record.

At the doorstep Polly laughed to herself—so soon does love forget its tragedies!—and was not permitted to take one step farther until she told what it was that seemed so funny. At first she wouldn't tell, but Chip has the name of being a persistent young man. So finally she said she was laughing at the sudden change in the weather. And she left Chip to figure that out for himself.

Center Point Publishing
600 Brooks Road ● PO Box 1
Thorndike ME 04986-0001 USA

(207) 568-3717

US & Canada:
1 800 929-9108